"Wow! You've got an electric grand piano," Adrian said, following Celeste into her living room.

"Since you own something this nice, it's probably redundant to ask if you play. Maybe we could do something together one day. I'd bring my guitar."

She broke out into a cold sweat. Her hand shook too much to put on the CD she'd chosen. Her past was behind her. What Adrian was asking was entirely different.

She forced the words out. "I just play for my own enjoyment. I don't think so." Her words were truer than Adrian would ever know. When she played for her own enjoyment, she now only played alone. She'd exchanged the joy of making music with others for something of far greater value...even if at times the loneliness hurt.

GAIL SATTLER

lives in Vancouver, British Columbia (where you don't have to shovel rain), with her husband of twenty-six years, three sons, two dogs, five lizards, one toad and a degu named Bess. Gail loves to read stories with a happy ending, which is why she writes them. Visit Gail's Web site at www.gailsattler.com.

HEARTS IN HARMONY

GAIL SATTLER

Steeple Hill®

Published by Steeple Hill Books™

STEEPLE HILL BOOKS

Steeple
Hill®

ISBN 0-373-87310-7

HEARTS IN HARMONY

www.SteepleHill.com

Printed in U.S.A.

Therefore, my brothers,
I want you to know that through Jesus
the forgiveness of sins is proclaimed to you.
—*Acts* 13:38

Dedicated to Colleen Coble, TD.
Without you, this wouldn't have been possible.
SD

Chapter One

The engine began to spit. The car chugged, slowed and died.

Celeste Hackett steered her mother's decrepit sedan onto the gravel shoulder of the deserted country road and came to a complete stop. The endless expanse of farmers' fields seemed to mock the silence of the dead car.

She refused to accept being stranded in the middle of nowhere.

Celeste attempted to restart the car, but the engine only made a horrid grinding sound, turning over and over with no contact.

With a groan, she lowered her head to the top of the steering wheel. She had been a fool to trade cars with her mother. She should have known her mother's hunk of junk wouldn't make the long trip back without something going wrong, but she tried to convince herself now that it was far better that her own reliable car was sitting in her mother's garage, ready for her mother to begin her vacation tomorrow, and that it was she, Celeste, who was stranded in the middle of nowhere. If the car couldn't make the shorter trip fifty miles between her home and her mother's home, it definitely wouldn't have made the fifteen-hundred-mile trip from her mother's home to her aunt's home, which was where her mother was going on an extended holiday.

Celeste now had two options. She could either walk ten miles ahead to the gas station at the highway entrance to ask for assistance, or thirty-five miles back to her mother's house where she could call for a tow truck.

At the thought of all that walking, Celeste gritted her teeth and whacked the top of the dashboard with her fist. The needle on the gas gauge quivered, then dropped to the E.

Celeste tried not to scream. Her mother had given her a list of the car's problems but apparently had forgotten to mention the malfunctioning gas gauge. However, if her mother knew about it, list, or not, there would be a container of gas in the trunk.

Celeste froze. Carrying a can of gas in the trunk was dangerous, but it was also dangerous for a woman to be stranded alone in the middle of nowhere.

Praying for the best, Celeste pushed the heavy door open, trying to ignore the creak of the rusty hinge. As she stepped onto the highway, a blast of heat hit her in the face. She did her best to ignore the stifling temperatures and walked to the rear of the car, where the stench of the car's last, fatal backfire caused her to cough painfully. Once she caught her breath, she jabbed the key in the trunk lock. After a series of calculated wiggles, a click sounded and the lock opened. When she hoisted the heavy lid of the trunk, gas fumes wafted up.

The gas can lay on its side. Beside it lay the plug for the container's air hole. She picked up the plastic container and shook it, confirming that it was indeed, empty.

Celeste squeezed her eyes shut for a brief second. Taking the short cut through the country rather than the longer but well-traveled main highway had not been a good choice.

She slammed the trunk shut. The bang echoed into oblivion over the surrounding fields, taunting her.

Grumbling under her breath, she replaced the plug to the empty gas container, pocketed the keys, hiked her purse strap over her shoulder, and began the long walk down the deserted country road.

Monday morning, she was going to buy a cell phone.

Adrian Braithwaite glanced at his watch and smiled. Despite the abundant potholes, the back road was still faster than the main route. And it was that knowledge that was going to earn him a big, fat, chocolate donut from his friend Paul after the evening service tonight. After he beat Paul home, of course.

An abandoned vehicle at the side of the road loomed up on the horizon. He slowed to stare. It was some car—a variety of different colors, one door blue, the trunk red, while the main body of the car was probably at one time supposed to have been white. The antenna was bent at a ridiculous angle, and the muffler was tied up with wire. The car's condition made him wonder if someone had bought it out of a junkyard, intending to restore the old beast, although he didn't think it was exactly a collector's item.

Adrian checked his watch again as he drove on. He could taste that donut already.

Although he could no longer see the old car, his thoughts returned to its absent owner. Now that he thought about it, the car probably belonged to a teenager, maybe a first car. Given the old car's condition, however, it was more likely, it belonged to someone down on their luck.

A few miles further, he caught sight of a person up ahead, walking on the shoulder, or rather, he caught sight of a gas can, its bright red visible far in the distance.

Adrian slowed again to study the stranded motorist. A green T-shirt and jeans covered a narrow waist and a nice feminine figure.

He frowned. Familiar stories of women alone being attacked or abducted flashed through his mind. He didn't want that to happen.

Expecting her to stick out her thumb to hitch a ride when she heard him coming, Adrian slowed even more, until he was parallel to her.

Not only did she not stick out her thumb, she didn't even look at him. Instead, she remained on the left shoulder, walking determinedly against oncoming traffic—if there had been any other traffic.

She appeared to be a couple of years younger than himself, probably about twenty-five, with chin length brunette hair, and a pert little nose. An understandable scowl tightened pouty lips. To attract her attention, Adrian leaned out the window as he idled along the highway.

He smiled. "Hi," he called across the empty lane. "Need a lift?"

A shiver of dread passed through Celeste. After walking for over an hour during the hottest part of the summer day, Celeste was tired beyond description, not to mention crabby. Her feet hurt, and her throat was so dry she thought she might soon dissolve into a little pile of dust.

Knowing the man was looking at her, Celeste didn't turn her head. Out of the corner of her eye, she tried to determine if she'd seen him before.

Without altering her brisk pace, Celeste turned her head slightly so she could see him better.

The man appeared respectable, which alone lessened the likelihood that he was someone she might have met before.

From what she could see, he was well-dressed and clean-shaven. His dark hair sported a stylish cut, even though it was mussed from driving with the window open. He wore what appeared to be prescription glasses with clip-ons for sunglasses. However, his friendly smile and pleasant baritone voice were not enough to make her trust him. She'd encountered smooth talkers before, one in particular, and paid for it dearly. She would never make that mistake again.

Celeste faced forward, not altering her steady pace. "No thanks, I'd rather walk."

The man kept smiling. "Are you sure? It's still five miles to the junction and the nearest gas station. Maybe more. I'm obviously going right past it."

Celeste groaned inwardly. She didn't want to become another statistic. On the surface, the man seemed okay, but then so did every creep who was later discovered to be a serial rapist or mass murderer.

While inconvenient, the walk itself wouldn't kill her.

"Thanks for the offer. I'll walk."

The man continued to drive beside her.

"Why is there never a cop around when you need one?"

she grumbled between her teeth. The empty plastic gas can was useless as a weapon, as was her purse. Slipping her fingers into her pocket, she withdrew her keys slowly and threaded a few between her fingers in case she had to stab him in self defense.

"My name's Adrian Braithwaite. What's yours?"

Celeste's heart pounded in her chest. She clenched her fingers harder around the keys. "Never mind," she snapped.

He pulled a bit ahead of her so she could see his face without turning her head, then leaned out the window as he continued to drive slowly. He flashed an infuriating smile. "Pleased to meet you, Miss Mind. Or may I call you Never?"

Celeste remained silent.

"Now that we've been formally introduced, would you like that ride? I assure you, I'm a responsible citizen, and I go to church faithfully every Sunday. I'm only concerned for your safety."

Celeste refused to acknowledge him. She'd been taken in before by tempting promises.

At her lack of response, he sat back properly in the car and fumbled with something beside him. One arm appeared out the window, and the car swerved close enough for her to take something out of his hand. "Here," he called out. "Take this. It's my cell phone. You can call my mother, she'll tell you what a nice guy I am. Her name is Mrs. Braithwaite, but you can call her Stella. We're already too far from your car to bother calling for a tow."

"No thank you," she mumbled, and kept walking.

The man shrugged his shoulders and retracted his arm.

"I can certainly understand if you're nervous. If you don't want to get in the car with me, can I drive beside you until you get to the gas station? I would really hate to read in the paper that something bad happened. I'd never be able to live with myself."

Celeste nearly stumbled at his words. She'd already developed a blister that had burst, making her deeply regret not taking the time to switch from pantyhose to soft plush socks when she'd changed from her dress to her jeans after church.

"Suit yourself," she mumbled. "Don't you have anything better to do?"

He checked his watch and sighed. "Not anymore."

A sudden breeze whipped up, blowing a lock of hair into her face. She spat it out and wiped her mouth with the back of her hand without missing a step.

"Nice weather we're having," he called out. "The weather report says it will be hot like this for four more days."

Celeste closed her eyes for a couple of steps. The heat was getting to her without his reminder. Not a cloud was in sight to offer any relief. The farmers' fields provided no trees for an occasional patch of shade. She couldn't decide what was worse to walk on, the uneven gravel of the shoulder, or the steaming hot, broken pavement.

To keep from tripping or walking away from her straight path, Celeste opened her eyes and trudged on. She'd never thought her purse particularly heavy, but after carrying it on her shoulder all this time, it felt as if it weighed a ton. She switched the gas can to her other hand to relieve her numb fingers, at the same time swiping her forearm across her sweaty forehead. She'd never been so thirsty in her life. "Yeah, nice weather," she grumbled.

"See the game on TV last night? Great, wasn't it?"

She wanted to turn and give him a dirty look, but she didn't want him to see her exhaustion.

"If you don't want to talk, how about if I turn up the music? Although you'd hear it better if you got in the car."

Celeste opened her mouth, about to reply, but snapped it shut again. She dearly wanted to accept the ride, but stubborn determination and self-preservation won. She valued her life.

She kept walking.

"I'll take that as a yes." He reached forward and turned up the volume. To Celeste's shock, one of the songs from her favorite praise album resounded through the open window.

She dearly wanted to trust him. Every step hurt. Her throat was so parched every bit of dust she kicked up while walking burned her dry throat.

For now, at least, the music was making the long walk slightly less intolerable. Despite the harsh dryness in her throat, Celeste found herself humming to her favorite parts, until they finally reached the gas station.

At the same time as Celeste filled her red container, the man topped up his tank. They walked into the building at the same time to pay. He headed straight to the cashier, but Celeste detoured to the cooler for a cold drink, allowing him to be first in line.

She placed the drink on the counter while he counted out his money to the clerk. At her height of five foot five with shoes, he towered above her. He had removed the clip-ons when they got inside, which allowed her to see friendly hazel eyes through his glasses. He remained silent as he paid the clerk. Judging from the paltry amount of money exchanged, he really hadn't needed any gas.

Celeste opened the drink and took a long sip before she spoke. "Thank you for keeping an eye on me and caring for my safety on the long road here. I really do appreciate it."

Adrian smiled and bowed his head. "You're welcome, Miss Mind. Always willing to help a lady in distress."

Not that she'd been in distress, but she supposed she could have been if another car with not such a nice driver had shown up on the deserted road. Now that she was safely at the gas station, Celeste could appreciate the thought.

He started to walk out, but stopped at the magazine rack. Instead of leaving, he picked up a magazine and started paging through it.

Celeste fished through her wallet while she spoke to the young attendant behind the counter. "Is there any way I could trouble you or any of the other staff for a ride back to my car? I would be happy to pay for the inconvenience."

"Sorry, lady," the young clerk replied with a shrug of his shoulders. "Like, I'm the only one here, you know, and I can't lock up and leave. My shift just started. If you need a ride I'd be happy to oblige you, but you gotta wait for my shift to end and Josh to get here."

Celeste contemplated her options. A cab would cost more money than she could afford, but she didn't have anyone she could call to come and get her. She certainly wasn't going to wait seven hours at the gas station for a ride.

Adrian appeared at her side. "I'll gladly give you a ride back to your car. What would it take to convince you that my intentions are indeed honorable?"

She stared up at him. Her mind went blank.

"I know…" His voice trailed off as he dug into his back pocket and pulled out his wallet. "Here."

Celeste automatically accepted what he gave her. It was his driver's license and a credit card.

"This proves I'm who I say I am. It's a bad picture, but that's me. See?" He frowned and closed one eye slightly more than the other to imitate a typical bad driver's license photo. "And that's my signature, right there. Besides, everyone at the gas station has seen us."

Celeste somehow doubted that mass murderers gained the trust of their victims with photo I.D. and a major credit card.

She smiled politely, resigned to her fate, while she read the information on the driver's license. The walk back would surely kill her anyway, even if Braithwaite, Adrian Andrew, single male, age twenty-nine, 185 pounds, six feet one inch tall, dark-brown hair, hazel eyes, didn't. "You win," she mumbled, trying to sound gracious. "I would be forever grateful if you could give me a ride back to the car."

They walked in silence to his car, where in gentlemanly fashion, he opened the passenger door for her, then closed it firmly when she was settled in her seat. When he entered the driver's side, Celeste pressed herself against the door and watched his every move.

He sighed as she continued to watch him. "Please, don't be so nervous. Let me show you I really am a decent human being." Instead of starting the car, Adrian reached between the seats, pulled out an envelope, and handed her the paper from inside. It was a phone bill.

"That's my mother's phone number. See how often I call her? You can even phone her yourself." Triumphantly, he retrieved the cellular phone from under his seat and offered it to her again.

Celeste scanned the bill, showing a number of charges to the same number. "This bill is overdue."

Adrian's smile faded as he snatched back the paper. "No it's not." He studied it further. "That's an old bill. See where I tore off the bottom part to mail it in?"

"How do I know it's your mother? I only have your word for it."

He shrugged his shoulders. "So then phone *your* mother." He handed her the phone, then reached in front of her and flipped open the glove compartment, revealing a jumble of papers stuffed so tightly she didn't know how the small compartment hadn't exploded. He pulled out a plastic envelope, quickly pushed the papers back, and slammed the door shut. "Here's my vehicle registration. You've already seen my driver's license. Phone your mother and tell her who you're with so if you go missing the cops will come and arrest me."

As she pressed the power button and waited for the phone to locate the signal, she could feel his eyes upon her.

Celeste didn't raise her head, only her eyes, and blatantly stared back. The privacy and confined quarters of his car allowed her to study his face closer than she had inside the gas station. He didn't turn away. He only smiled, openly inviting her scrutiny.

Even with him looking right back, she couldn't stop staring. Up close, his hazel eyes seemed more than friendly. They radiated sincerity and kindness. While he wasn't exactly movie-star handsome, he wasn't bad.

Summoning all her self control, she forced herself to quit staring and switched her attention to the phone. Quickly, she punched in her mother's phone number, then held the phone up to her ear until it made the connection. While she waited she looked back up at Adrian.

He hadn't moved. It suddenly occurred to her that while she had been studying him, he had been studying her. As soon as their eyes met, he crossed his arms and leaned back in his seat, almost as if he could tell she needed more space.

Despite the fact that he'd been nothing but a perfect gentleman, her insides still quivered and she remained tense, ready to open the door and run.

"It's busy. I guess I'll just have to trust you."

While Adrian started the engine, Celeste reminded herself that although it had taken hours to walk here, they would be back at her mother's car in approximately ten minutes. However, by the time they reached it, Celeste was filled with guilt at having been so rotten to him. He had remained with her to ensure her safety, and now he was going out of his way to help her again.

He watched from a respectable distance as Celeste stood beside the gas cap and fumbled with the opening to the gas can.

She didn't raise her head as she spoke. "I really appreciate all your help," she mumbled, "especially after I was so rude when you were only trying to be nice."

He answered her with a humorless smile. "Don't worry about it. I understand. I'm glad I was able to help. You must be tired after that long walk."

"Yes. Pride has its price."

After a few chugs and a puff of black smoke, the car started. She rolled the window down and leaned out. "Thanks again, Adrian,"

"You're welcome. Any time."

She pulled onto the highway and watched in the rear-view mirror as Adrian drove behind her. She stopped at the same gas station she'd just been at minutes ago, and waved at Adrian as he continued past.

It took so long to fill the car's large gas tank that Celeste nearly fell asleep on her feet. However, when the pump clicked off to indicate the tank was finally full, the amount of money on the display jolted her to full wakefulness.

As she walked into the building once again and waited in line to pay, she tried to calculate how much more her mother's sorry excuse for a car would cost while her mother was gone.

"I see you're back. Anything else you need?"

Celeste shook her head and pulled her wallet out of her purse. Since she didn't have that much cash on her, she was forced to charge the amount. As she ran her fingers over the slots in her wallet to pull out her credit card, her hand froze.

Tucked neatly in her wallet were Adrian Braithwaite's driver's license and credit card.

Chapter Two

In the privacy of her kitchen, Celeste surveyed Adrian's driver's license.

Even though she hadn't lived in the neighborhood very long, she recognized his address as two blocks east and three streets north from her own rented duplex. Before she'd moved in, she'd checked out the neighborhood. She had probably even driven past his house. He lived that close.

Celeste shook her head. She had to return his things. Immediately. Just in case he hadn't gone straight home, Celeste gathered up her courage, looked up the number, and dialed.

"Hello?" Adrian's deep baritone voice answered.

She sucked in a deep breath to compose herself. "Hi. This is Celeste."

"Who? I think you have the wrong number."

"No! Adrian, don't hang up. It's me, Miss Never Mind."

"Miss Never…" His voice trailed off. Silence hung over the line for a few seconds before he continued. "So now I know your name, Celeste. You made it home safely, I assume?"

A nervous laugh escaped. "I seem to have accidentally kept your driver's license and credit card. I'm so embarrassed, and so sorry. Can I come over to return them to you?"

"I don't know if I'd trust that car if I were you. If you want I can come over to your place and pick them up."

As nice as he seemed, she didn't want him to know where she lived. For now, she wanted to settle into her new home the same way she was settling into her new job—only concerning herself with what directly affected her. "I'm actually not very far away at the moment. Besides, it's illegal to drive without your license on hand. It's no trouble. It's the least I can do."

"As long as you're sure. Do you need directions?"

"No, I know where it is. I'll be there in a few minutes."

"You do? Well, okay See you soon. Bye."

Celeste tried to push back her nervousness as she hung up the phone. He sounded exactly the same on the phone as he did in person—friendly and likeable, but she was still going to take her own car rather than walk, so she could make a fast getaway.

She couldn't remember ever meeting someone who could be so helpful to a stranger when there was nothing in it for them. She wished she had met him at a different point in time. If she had, her life might have been entirely different now.

But that was just foolishness. Nothing would change her past, or who it had made her. All she could do was continue on, and hope her past would never catch up with her future.

As she walked from the house to the car, Celeste studied her new neighborhood. The houses were older and fairly small, but well-cared for. Most of the people made tending the grass and flowers in their yards weekend projects. A few of her neighbors had waved at her as she hurried by, recognizing her as her landlord, Hank's new tenant.

She smiled and breathed the fresh green scents deeply. This neighborhood had been a good choice for a new beginning, everything was beautiful and taken care of with pride.

The only ugly thing here was her mother's car.

Gritting her teeth, she pulled the car door open, hoping the creaking hinge didn't draw too much attention, and slid in. The four-wheeled monstrosity started with a chug and a backfire, but it did start. Celeste arrived at Adrian's house in under two minutes.

Adrian lived in a small brightly painted bungalow with a well-kept yard. Celeste recognized his shiny black car in the driveway. Beside his car sat a small sporty blue model.

Taking a deep breath for courage, Celeste knocked on the front door and waited.

A deep male voice called from inside. "Hey! Adrian! There she is!"

The door opened. Adrian stood tall in the doorway as he smiled down at her. In the middle of the living room stood a rather handsome blond man about the same age. The man smiled as well and cocked his head to one side.

Celeste squirmed. She felt strange enough with Adrian looking at her. She didn't want to be analyzed by his friend, although she didn't know why she cared. After today, she would never see him again.

"Hi, Celeste. Or should I say Miss Mind?" Adrian grinned. She could see his eyes focusing over her shoulder, taking in her mother's scrap heap of a car parked on the street.

Celeste lowered her head and quickly reached into her pocket for his license and credit card. "I'm really sorry about this. Thanks again for your concern this afternoon. Bye."

Without giving him a chance to respond, she shoved the two cards into his hand, turned and ran back to the car.

"Wait!" Adrian's voice sounded from behind her.

The second she inserted the key into the ignition, he appeared at the car door. With her heart in her throat and grateful for the shelter of the car, Celeste rolled the window down at the same time as she started the engine.

Adrian ducked his head toward her. "May I see you again?"

Celeste had to force herself to breathe. She would have been a fool if she didn't know what he wanted. She wasn't ready for that kind of relationship. She wanted to trust him, but she didn't know if she had it in her to do so. Maybe she never would. But even if she did, for now, she still needed time to hide and lick her wounds.

Celeste cleared her throat. "I don't think so, but I'm flattered that you asked."

Adrian stiffened and stepped back, ramming his hands into his pockets. "I had to try. Take care of yourself, Celeste. If you ever need a hand again, you know where to find me."

She drove away subdued. She didn't want to live her life as a recluse—that wasn't why she had moved so far from all that was familiar. However, meeting new people had turned out to be much more difficult than she thought it would be. The people she met at her new job were safe, because she would only see them at work. But this was different. Starting something with Adrian, even if it was only friendship, was too close to home. Literally.

When she pulled in front of her house, Celeste didn't get out of the car. She turned off the engine and stared at the home that had been hers for only four days. God had provided a way for her to start again—she had a new job and a new place to live. She'd also prayed for God to send her some new friends, people she could trust and with whom she could be safe.

God had put what had appeared to be a trustworthy man in her path, but she'd let fear get the best of her. He'd offered what could be the beginning of a friendship, and she'd turned and run. Now she couldn't go back without looking desperate.

Celeste lowered her forehead to the top of the steering wheel and shut her eyes.

God, I'm so sorry. I said I trusted You, but I blew it. I couldn't do it. But I really need a friend, I really do. The next time You show me someone I can trust, I promise I'll give them the benefit of the doubt, just because I know You're giving me what I asked for, and You know best.

Celeste sighed, picked up her purse, and went inside.

First she'd promised God, and now she promised herself that the next time God provided an answer, she would listen.

Adrian strummed the last chord of the final song for the service. As the pastor approached the microphone, Adrian placed his guitar on the stand. Along with Paul, Bob and Randy, his friends on the worship team, he quietly exited the stage.

Every Sunday he sat with his friends during the pastor's sermon, but this time, when they shuffled into their usual seats near the front, Adrian kept walking.

During the short break when the children had been dismissed into Sunday School, he'd done a quick double-take as he looked into the congregation. Sitting almost at the back, if he wasn't mistaken, he'd seen Miss Never Mind.

He'd been thinking about her all week. She'd hummed along to his favorite CD. For a couple of the songs, she'd actually mouthed the words to the choruses. That meant she'd heard them before, often enough to repeat them.

He'd taken it as a sign from God when she finally got inside the car. But then, the tiny tiger who had walked for hours rather than get in the car had turned into a frightened rabbit. He'd been almost afraid to look at her, for fear that she would fling herself out the door at fifty-five miles an hour to get away. He'd ended up chattering like a dripping tap, just so there wouldn't be silence in the car.

Things hadn't gone any better when she'd showed up at his door. She'd disappeared so fast he was beginning to wonder if something was wrong with him.

Now, here she was in church. He felt as though God was giving him another chance.

As he approached, her eyes fixed on him.

She wore a nice skirt and blouse with matching shoes, a far cry from the dusty jeans, T-shirt and battered sneakers she'd worn the last time he'd seen her. Some kind of pink fabric thing that matched her blouse adorned her hair. But what really made him take notice was the Bible beside her.

He stopped, then crouched down to speak to her. "Hi, Celeste. It's great to see you here today. Is this seat taken?"

Her pretty eyes widened at the question, holding his attention with their vivid jade-green color.

In the blink of an eye, she lowered her head, scooped

up her Bible and the bulletin and stiffened. Her voice came out in a tight squeak. "No, it's not taken."

At the first scripture reading during the sermon, Adrian leaned closer to Celeste. "I left my Bible up at the front with my friends. Can I peek at yours?"

She paged to the correct passage and held her Bible between them. He could have read it better if it hadn't been shaking so much, but Adrian didn't dare move to steady it.

During the sermon, he tried his best to pay attention to the pastor's words, but Celeste's presence distracted him.

She was still scared of him. He wanted to know why, but this wasn't the time to discuss it, not in the middle of the service. However, if he waited till it was over, he'd be back up front, with the worship team, and she would be out the door before he had a chance to find out what was wrong.

When Pastor Ron drew his sermon to a close, just before everyone was instructed to bow their heads for the closing prayer, Adrian touched Celeste's arm. He tried not to feel hurt when she flinched. "Please," he whispered as he leaned closer to her. "I'd like to talk to you after the service. I have to go up to the front now for the closing hymn. Promise me you'll wait. Don't be so nervous. I don't bite."

Her eyes drifted to the front, then back to him. "All right," she whispered.

He was the last one to arrive at the front, and he played terribly. Paul kept turning away from the congregation and toward him, going as far as nodding his head in rhythm to get Adrian to slow his tempo to match everyone else.

Adrian fought to slow his pace, repeating in his head that the music was to help everyone in the congregation center their thoughts on God; they didn't want to be distracted by an impatient guitar player.

Still, instead of watching his music, he watched Celeste. The closer they got to the end of the song, the more Celeste kept glancing at the door. On the last repeat of the chorus, she began shuffling in her chair.

After the last chord, Pastor Ron closed the service and dismissed the congregation. Adrian should have kept playing as the sanctuary emptied, but he dropped his guitar into the holder and walked off as his friends stared at him. This time, he couldn't let her get away.

He arrived beside Celeste just as she tucked her bulletin inside her Bible. Her purse was already slung over her shoulder. All the bravado he'd worked up dissolved into a little puddle at his feet.

She looked up at him. "I really enjoyed the service. Your pastor is quite a dynamic speaker."

Adrian nodded. A neutral topic. Perfect. "Yes, he is. Since this is your first time here, I'd love to introduce you to him."

"Maybe another time. I think it's time for me to leave."

Adrian stepped aside, but he couldn't let her go. He cleared his throat. "If you're not busy, why don't you join me for lunch? My treat. So we can talk."

The chatter, background music, the scraping of chairs, and the voices of little children echoed behind Adrian, but between the two of them, the silence was almost tangible. She looked up into his eyes and studied his face as he'd never been studied before.

Finally, she gave him a weak smile. "That would be nice. I'm new to the area and obviously new to this church. I do have some questions."

He tried not to appear too eager or too relieved. "Great. I just have to go get my guitar before we leave."

Back on the stage, Adrian mumbled a quick apology for not helping pack up the sound system, slipped his guitar into the case and hurried away.

This time, Celeste's old car was running fine, and she insisted on meeting him at the restaurant. Since he'd left the building sooner than he'd ever left before, they arrived before most of the regular church crowd, and got a table right away.

The waitress quickly took their orders and left them with a decanter of coffee. Adrian folded his hands on the table, and smiled at Celeste. "Welcome to the neighborhood. I think you'll like it here. It's very peaceful. The residents are mostly people who have owned the same homes for years and have retired here, or younger families starting out with their first home."

She nodded. "That sounds nice. Have you lived here long?"

"It depends what you call 'long'. I bought my house five years ago, and I'm still here. Maybe I'll be the next generation to stay until I retire."

"What about your church? What's it like?"

Adrian smiled politely. He felt more as though he was being interviewed than having a friendly chat. At least now, unlike a week ago, Celeste was talking openly. Interview or not, anything was better than the scared rabbit she'd been last time they talked.

"It's a good church, with good people, good fellowship and the pastor delivers a strong message. It's a church plant, started from the big church where I grew up, not far from here. We've only been in this building a few months, but I guess I've been with the same crowd all my life. As I understand it, my mother brought me to my first service at the parent church when I was one month old. I became a Christian when I was twelve. When they started the church plant, the associate pastor at the old church, who is now the only pastor here, asked me and my friends if we would go with the core group and put together a worship team, because we all grew up together in the church and all play an instrument."

Her eyes widened. "Wow… You've been a Christian for seventeen years. And always been with the same people."

He almost asked how she figured out the time frame, but then he remembered she'd been in possession of his driver's license. The math was easy. He tried not to be flattered that she'd memorized his birthday.

"For the most part, yes, it's really been a great church family. All of us guys on the worship team grew up in this neighborhood. We've been together all our lives, except Paul, briefly. He moved away for a while, but came back. Do you remember him? He was at my house when you dropped by with my driver's license."

Celeste nodded. "Yes. He's the one who plays the bass guitar right?"

"Bob and Randy live close by, too. Bob's the drummer. He's as Italian as he looks." Adrian grinned, thinking of his friend. "But don't tell Bob I said that."

Her eyes widened, and Adrian hoped he hadn't given her the wrong impression. All the guys teased Bob endlessly with jokes about his large family and ethnic roots, but Bob, being Bob, took it all in stride.

"Randy's the one on the keyboard. I should probably warn you about him."

"Warn me? Why?"

"He tends to fool around a lot, and most people don't take him seriously, but he's a great guy. He just needs to settle down a bit."

Since he'd mentioned Bob's ethnicity, he tried to think of some way to set Randy apart. If he had to narrow it down to one thing, he would have said that Randy's most striking feature was his blue eyes. Personally, Adrian didn't think Randy's eyes were a big deal, but women seemed to be drawn to them. That was exactly the reason he was not going to draw Celeste's attention to Randy's big baby blues. Besides, Randy was just… Randy.

"That's so nice that you and your friends are on the worship team together. I hope you don't mind me asking, but what do you do for a living?"

Now, more than ever, he felt as if he was being interviewed.

Adrian stiffened. "Actually, my job is changing. Last year they promoted me to management, and they're changing my job description again, so I don't know what I should call myself."

She kept staring at him. Fortunately, before she had the chance to ask him anything else, the waitress appeared with their lunches.

Adrian folded his hands in front of him on the table. "Would you like me to lead with a word of prayer before we eat?"

She turned her head from side to side, taking in the people at all the nearby tables. "Here? In a restaurant? You would do that?"

Adrian's mouth opened, but no words came out. He'd never thought about not praying just because he was in a public setting.

Before he could think of something to say, she broke out into a wide smile. "I think that's a great idea."

Abruptly, she folded her hands in front of her on the table, bowed her head, closed her eyes and waited.

Adrian's mind went blank. He cleared his throat to give himself time to compose his thoughts.

"Thank you, dear Lord, for the food we're about to eat. Thank you also for new friends with whom we can share. I ask for Your continued blessings in the name of our Savior Jesus Christ. Amen."

He'd barely finished his first bite of fries when Celeste started again with the questions. "If you came with the same people from the other church, and you've been attending for so long, this must be a really nice group of people. Stable and everything? No surprises?"

Adrian nodded while he swallowed his mouthful. "I've got an idea. If you actually want to meet some of the people, rather than just sitting next to them, come to the evening service. Attendance is always lower, but it's a great opportunity to talk in a more relaxed setting. If you're nervous, I could pick you up."

Time stretched on forever as she glanced at him, then over his shoulder to the door, then back to him.

"I've never been to an evening church service; that sounds like a good idea, but if you don't mind, I think I'll take my own car."

Adrian felt his smile drop, but he quickly forced it back. He tried to convince himself that it was better she came on her own, because he had to be early to set up and practice. However, unless he picked her up, he couldn't be assured she would actually go. He hoped she would keep her promise.

They made pleasant small talk for the remainder of lunch. When they went their separate ways in their separate cars, Adrian couldn't help but smile. She'd been careful to avoid telling him exactly where she lived, but he knew her car. He couldn't miss that eyesore of a vehicle, no matter where it was, unless she parked it in the garage every single time she got home.

Starting Monday, it would be a good time to change his route when he took out his bicycle. Instead of the bike trail at the park, he might just cruise the neighborhood. Slowly.

But for now, he had never anticipated attending the evening service so much.

Celeste walked into the foyer quietly. Instead of standing alone in the growing crowd, she made her way immediately to the sanctuary. She sat in approximately the same place she had that morning and waited for the service to begin. She'd only been sitting a couple of minutes when Adrian looked up at her and smiled brightly.

Easily recognizing the other men from Adrian's descriptions, she watched them as they practiced, but she paid the most attention to Randy, the one on the keyboard.

Randy seemed to be the only one obviously having fun. He would try different things, and with trying something new, he often made a mistake. Whenever that happened, Adrian also made a mistake, and then they both did the worst thing musicians in a group could do—they both paused at the same time in the middle of a song. Every time that happened, Paul, the bass guitarist, shut his eyes and kept playing until they recovered, while Bob, the drummer, struggled not to laugh. Randy would shrug his shoulders, play what he was supposed to for just a little while, then the cycle would start again.

Watching Randy on the keyboard sent a wave of longing through Celeste. Randy wasn't bad. He was just a little too adventurous for his own good.

She shook her head and turned away.

She was in church to worship God, the God who had pulled her out of the pit. She wasn't here to critique the band.

To distract herself, Celeste turned her attention to the others in the sanctuary. Almost everyone there was close to her own age. The evening crowd was about a third of the number who attended the morning service. Hardly any children were present. The majority of the people wore jeans, including the men of the worship team. Even the pastor was dressed casually. There wasn't a tie to be seen in the entire crowd.

What appeared to be the youth group occupied an entire section. In keeping with the informal setting, the worship team played only contemporary music, making Celeste guess the evening service was geared to the teens and young adults.

Adrian and all his friends, this time, joined her during the pastor's message, though they all returned to the front for the closing. The second the pastor announced coffee and donuts at the back, most of the seats in the church emptied.

It didn't take Adrian long to appear at her side.

"If you want a donut, you'd better hurry. The youth group gets them pretty fast. Sometimes, it's a real free-for-all."

Adrian's friendly smile did little to quell her rising uneasiness. All he was doing was offering her a donut, and nothing more. She really was trying to follow what she thought was God's direction. Adrian could have been a poster child for trustworthiness. Unlike her, he was stable enough to have bought his own house as a single man, while she was barely in a position to rent. He worked at a job he'd had for a long time. He even visited his mother often.

Since they'd parted that afternoon, Celeste had told herself over and over that all he'd been was…nice. He'd given her no reason to doubt his sincerity, and no reason to think he was anything other than what he appeared to be.

Adrian escorted her to the back. No one approached them, although she did notice a few people taking second glances, as she was probably the only stranger in their midst.

She had just bitten into a powdered sugar donut when the other three men from the worship team circled around her.

Randy, the man who had played the keyboard, stepped closer. "What's a nice girl like you doing in a place like this?" he asked as he waggled his eyebrows.

Celeste nearly choked on her donut. When she'd first told people she knew that she'd started attending church, everyone had asked her the same question, except no one called her nice. Celeste tried her best to wipe the powdered sugar from her mouth discreetly.

Adrian sighed. "Celeste, I'd like you to meet my friends. Except if they keep it up, they won't be my friends for much longer." He paused. No one refuted him, so he continued. "This is Randy."

Again, Randy grinned. Celeste had never seen such an adorable boyish grin on a man his age, and Randy's blue eyes were positively striking.

"I believe you saw Paul briefly at my house."

The tall blond man nodded politely. "Charmed," he said, and his expression made her think he actually meant it.

Celeste felt herself blushing, something she hadn't done for many years. It felt strange.

"And this is Bob."

The drummer's eyes narrowed slightly as he studied her. "I don't believe I've ever seen you here before. Welcome to Faith Community Fellowship. It's good to have you here."

Celeste had enjoyed the morning service, but to be seeing everyone just being themselves completely melted away her worries. Some teens were squabbling over the last donut and all the adults were in small groups, laughing and talking. From the volume of the chatter and laughter, Celeste could barely believe she was in a church.

Randy turned his head toward the front, and then back again. "Hey, Adrian. We've got all our stuff cleaned up. Maybe you should do the same. At least wind your patch cord and knock down your stands."

Adrian smiled. "Excuse me, Celeste. I'll only be a few minutes."

As Adrian left, another man joined them. Randy introduced him as Pastor Ron.

Celeste had never spoken to a real live pastor before. He wasn't at all like she expected. He seemed so…ordinary.

When the pastor excused himself, a few more people from the congregation joined them, and Randy introduced them one by one. Before long, she'd talked to so many people she couldn't remember their names.

By the time Adrian returned, the crowd was thinning. Randy noticed the same thing, and whispered to her that it was because the donuts were gone.

Celeste couldn't help herself. She liked Randy. In fact, she liked all of Adrian's friends. She couldn't remember the last time she'd enjoyed a day so much, if she ever had. Most important, she couldn't remember the last time she'd actually been able to relax in a crowd.

Unfortunately, with relaxation came tiredness. Paul caught her stifling a yawn.

"Excuse me," she muttered between her fingers. "I don't know why I'm suddenly so tired. I should go, anyway. I have to be up early for work in the morning."

Almost in unison, Adrian, Bob, Randy and Paul checked their watches, and Adrian said, "Let me walk you to your car."

She said her good-byes and made her way out with Adrian at her side.

He waited patiently while she struggled to get the key turned in the lock the right way to open the car door.

"Thank you for a lovely day, Adrian."

"You're more than welcome. I hope to see you again soon."

She nodded and quickly scooted into the car. "Yes," she mumbled as she pulled the door hard enough to force it closed. "You'll see me next Sunday morning. Bye."

Chapter Three

Celeste shut down her computer. It had been a busy day at work and she would have liked nothing better than to go home and put her feet up, but the fridge and cupboards were bare. Knowing she wouldn't have the energy to go out again after she'd settled down for the evening, she headed out to pick up her groceries on the way home.

List in hand, she trudged through the store. As soon as she had everything she needed in her grocery cart, she proceeded to the checkouts. One look at the long lines nearly made her groan out loud. At the same second she pushed her cart into what she hoped was the shortest line, a male voice sounded behind her.

"Hey, Celeste, fancy meeting you here."

Her breath caught and her hand shot up to her throat as she spun around. She nearly sank to the floor with relief that it wasn't anyone too familiar. "Adrian, you startled me. What are you doing here?"

He nodded at her shopping cart. "Same thing as you, apparently."

His cart contained more than double the volume of her own.

She counted the people in the line ahead of her. "It looks like we're going to be a while."

"On your way home from work?"

"Yes. I guess you are, too," she replied.

He nodded, but didn't speak.

She tried to guess what he did for a living. His clothes didn't give her an easy answer. Today, he wore tailored slacks that looked as though they belonged with a suit jacket, which he wasn't wearing, a good-quality cotton dress shirt and a tie. She knew his job was in management, but she didn't know what he managed. Obviously it wasn't something that required manual labor or a uniform.

She turned her attention back up to his face. He was grinning. "I knew you were here. I saw your car."

Her face flamed. She'd parked her mother's car in the back corner of the lot, next to the garbage bin, far away from everyone else, in an effort to escape notice.

She didn't want to hear that she could be so easily found. She tried to console herself by thinking no one she used to know would associate her with her mother's car, even if they did see it. Her own car was by now halfway across the country with her mother in it.

"If you really must know, it's my mother's car, not mine. We traded so she could have something safe to drive on her vacation. She left last week."

Adrian's smile dropped. "It sounds like that old thing isn't very dependable."

"It's not like it's going to blow up or anything. The worst that will happen is it will stall." She patted her purse.

"If that happens, I got a cell phone on my lunch break today. All I have to do is call a tow truck."

One eyebrow rose, but he said nothing.

The line moved them to the point where she had to begin unloading her groceries onto the conveyor belt. Having the length of the buggy between them made it impossible to talk softly, thus ending their conversation, which Celeste regretted. It had been so long since she'd had such a pleasant conversation about nothing in particular, she'd forgotten just how good it could be.

Adrian's deep voice interrupted her mental meanderings. "That's my favorite kind of ice cream. Do you share?"

She fumbled with the ice cream tub, then thunked it down before she dropped it. "I think it's in the Ten Commandments somewhere that you're not supposed to covet thy neighbor's ice cream."

He covered his stomach with his hands. "I haven't had dinner yet. That ice cream is too tempting for me. What about you? Have you had dinner? We could go out somewhere."

Celeste focused intently on unloading the remainder of her groceries onto the conveyor. "Sorry, not this time. There's stuff I have to put in the freezer. Like this ice cream, for example."

"I have an idea. I've got a frozen pizza. We can both go to your house, and you can put your groceries away. Then we can eat my pizza for supper, and your ice cream for dessert."

"Frozen pizza?" Celeste hesitated, then placed the last of her groceries onto the conveyor belt. After praying about the situation with Adrian all week, she'd decided to trust that God really had sent her a potential friend. However, she wasn't sure she was ready to open up the private sanctuary of her home.

But she had to eat.

When she was a teen and still living at home with her mother, Celeste had often had her girlfriends over for frozen pizza. The food had been horrible, but the evenings were fun.

Adrian wasn't exactly one of her cheerleading buddies, but Celeste knew she needed a little fun.

She tried to smile, but thought it probably looked as fake as it felt. "I haven't had a frozen pizza for years. Are they still just as bad?"

Adrian nodded very seriously. "Yes. I bought extra cheese."

"In that case, I can't refuse."

They chatted very little as the clerk processed their orders, and soon they were at her car.

"You parked beside me."

"Yeah. I did, didn't I?"

Her heart pounded. Adrian wasn't Zac. So far, at least, Adrian was harmless. He was on the worship team at his church, which went partway to proving that he was a dedicated Christian. Most of all, he'd gone out of his way to help her, more than once, demanding nothing in return.

She told herself she was being unreasonable. Adrian had no idea what was happening in her life, or what *had* happened, and he didn't need ever to know. He was only acting in a way that was natural for him, and she couldn't fault him for that.

She tried to keep her hand from shaking as she inserted the key into the lock, then wiggled it enough to get it to turn. She swung the back door open and was about to start loading her groceries, when Adrian's hand rested on her arm, halting her on the spot. She bit her lip so she wouldn't scream.

"That looks heavy. Can I help you with that?"

Without waiting for an answer, he stepped in front of her, reached into her cart, and began piling everything up on the back seat. "Most people put their groceries in the trunk," he mumbled as he worked.

"The trunk smells like gasoline."

His brows knotted as he frowned. "Maybe you should have that looked at."

"No, the gas container just spilled. It's nothing. I just have to remember to leave it open to air out next weekend. Actually, if I ever took this thing in to get fixed, they'd either bury it, or take all my money to fix it up. Besides, I only need to put up with it until my mother gets back. She keeps telling me she's going to have it restored, but somehow that never happens. Instead, it just keeps getting worse."

He nodded and continued to load all her groceries into the back seat without being asked.

Celeste stood back as her throat clogged. What he was doing obviously wasn't a big deal to him, but it was a big deal to her. Again, he was helping her, without thinking, without being asked, and without expecting anything in return.

She didn't know much about signs from God, yet she wondered if God was trying to tell her something.

He pushed the door closed, but the rusty hinge creaked and groaned, preventing the latch from catching properly. He re-opened it and slammed it shut, giving the handle a pensive wiggle.

"Are you sure this thing is safe to drive? I couldn't help but hear the grinding it made on Sunday when you left the parking lot."

"It's okay for short distances, which is all I have to do. Really, once it starts, it's fine after a couple of blocks."

His mouth opened and he raised one finger in the air, readying Celeste for what she thought would be a challenge to her decision, but nothing came out. The finger dropped, he stiffened, and he cleared his throat.

"Never mind. As soon as I put my own groceries in my trunk, we can be on our way. Just remember I have to follow you. You know where I live, but I don't know which house is yours."

While Adrian tossed his groceries into the trunk of his car, Celeste slid behind the wheel and closed her eyes to think and pray.

She still wasn't sure she was doing the right thing by encouraging Adrian in whatever it was he thought he was doing by being so friendly. However, she couldn't live underground like a gopher, only going to work and back. All she could do was count on Jesus for wisdom, guidance, strength, and protection and pray that she was doing the right thing. With her Savior by her side, she prayed she wouldn't make the same mistake twice.

The bang of Adrian's trunk closing made her eyes open. As she headed for home with Adrian behind her, she told herself that it was unrealistic to think she could keep where she lived secret. As far as risks went, being with Adrian out in public seemed a minimal one. At home, since she lived in a duplex, if she screamed, her landlord Hank would hear, and, she hoped, call the police.

Like a gentleman, Adrian helped Celeste carry all her groceries into the house. He disappeared while she tucked most of it away, then returned with one more bag.

"Would you mind putting this in your freezer? Everything else will be okay in the trunk, but this stuff has to stay frozen. I didn't think of it until now."

When she took the bag from his hand, he laid a frozen pizza on the table, along with a package of shredded mozzarella cheese, as promised.

He looked apologetic. "I don't usually eat like this, but I didn't feel like cooking today."

While Celeste made coffee, Adrian made a great show of ripping away the wrap from the pizza, and carefully sprinkling on the mozzarella cheese, making it look as though he was doing more work than it really required.

When the pizza was in the oven, Celeste walked into the living room to put some music on. She didn't have much yet, but she had started a small collection of Christian music, which included the same CD Adrian had had in his car.

While she tried to think of which one to put on, Adrian wandered across her living room.

"Wow. You've got a great electric piano. It's probably silly of me to ask if you play. Maybe we could do something together one day. I'd bring my guitar."

She broke out into a cold sweat. Her hand shook too much to put on the CD. Her past was behind her. What Adrian was asking was entirely different.

She forced the words out. "I just play for my own enjoyment. I don't think so." Her words were truer than Adrian could ever guess. When she said 'for her own enjoyment,' she meant she played alone. She'd exchanged the joy of making music with others for something of much more value, even if at times it hurt.

He fumbled for the switch, turned it on, and plunked out a few notes. "Nice sound. I tried to learn to play piano when I was a kid. I wasn't very good. I'm actually not very good on guitar, either, but I'm the best they've got." He plunked out a few more notes, shook his head and stepped back. "Would you like to tickle the ivories for me?"

"Plastics," she mumbled.

"Plastics?"

"The keys are plastic. Even if it was a real piano, I don't think they use ivory anymore."

He stared at her for a few seconds. "Then would you like to tickle the plastics?" Adrian paused as he shook his head. "I think it loses something when you say it that way."

Thankfully, she heard the oven timer go off. Before he could ask again, Celeste hustled into the kitchen, removed the pizza from the oven, cut it into slices, and set it on the table.

They bowed their heads while Adrian prayed. *"Dear Lord, thank You for this food, and for the rich blessings You've bestowed upon us. Thank You also for friends, both old and new, and the opportunity to share with them. Amen."*

She hadn't taken her first bite when Adrian started with the phrase she had been hoping wouldn't come out.

"So. Tell me a little about yourself."

Celeste studied her plate as she spoke. "There isn't much to tell. I work in the credit department of a small company. I haven't been there very long. Soon I'm going to take an accounting course. I've started looking into what's available at night school, so I can still work."

The touch of his hand on hers startled her. "See what

we have in common already? I'm an accountant. Also, we like the same ice cream."

What he was trying to do was more than obvious. While she did like him, she was far from ready to enter the relationship he alluded to.

He grinned. "You're looking at me funny."

"Sorry. You don't look like an accountant."

One eyebrow quirked. "And what should an accountant look like?"

Celeste chewed on her lower lip before answering. "Accountants are short and bald, wear suits all the time, and have suspenders to keep their pants up. They also have those little half-sized reading glasses perched on the ends of their noses all the time."

Adrian cleared his throat, straightened his stylish glasses, then ran his fingers through his hair. "I'll never be bald." He patted the knot of his tie. "Have I just been insulted?"

She shook her head. "No. I'm sorry. That came out wrong." Although her supervisor did look exactly as she'd described.

He let her steer the conversation away from personal questions and back to neutral topics. Before long she found herself enjoying his company and laughing at his lame jokes. When he checked his watch and stood to leave, her disappointment surprised her.

"I can't believe what time it is. The guys are coming over to practice tonight, and I have to get my groceries put away before they get there."

She escorted him to the door.

"Goodnight, Celeste. Will I see you again on Sunday? I'd like to pick you up, but I have to go early to set up."

Her answer came without thought. "Yes, I'll be there."

"I'll be looking forward to Sunday more than ever, then."

Adrian smiled and left.

After his car had rounded the corner, Celeste returned to the kitchen to clean up. However, when she entered the kitchen and looked at the fridge, she skidded to a halt.

Adrian had forgotten his bag of groceries in her freezer.

Without hesitation, she grabbed the bag, and ran out to coax her mother's car to start.

Three cars were parked in Adrian's driveway. Adrian's car was on the street, telling her that his friends had arrived before him.

Bag in hand, Celeste headed up the sidewalk.

Paul Calloway leaned against the corner of Adrian's table. He crossed his arms and watched his friend shoving his groceries into the cupboards with no concern for organization.

"I can't believe you forgot we moved up the practice time. In fact, it was your idea."

"I was busy with something else," Adrian mumbled, but didn't elaborate.

Adrian measured some coffee beans into the grinder, then filled the coffee machine with water. "You know, I'm positive I'm missing something. I'm sure I bought more than this."

The doorbell rang. Paul looked back over his shoulder. "You expecting someone?"

Adrian checked his watch, and shook his head. "No, I'm not. I'm kind of busy. Can you get that?"

Paul left Adrian in the kitchen and answered the door.

"Celeste? It's good to see you again. What are you doing here?"

"This is Adrian's. He forgot it. It's got to go in the freezer."

Paul couldn't hide his grin. He didn't know what was going on or why Celeste had Adrian's groceries, but he intended to find out.

"He's in the kitchen. Come on in."

Paul wished he had a camera to catch the expression on Adrian's face the moment Adrian saw Celeste in his kitchen. More than ever, it made Paul wonder what was going on. He'd never met Celeste before Sunday, nor had Adrian ever mentioned her, which made him even more curious.

Adrian recovered quickly. He mumbled a quick thank you as he accepted the bag from Celeste, and shoved it into the freezer.

Paul crossed his arms and turned to Celeste. "How did you like the services on Sunday? It was nice to see you there."

"I really like Faith Community Fellowship. I'm looking for a new church home, but I guess Adrian already told you that."

"Actually, no. He didn't."

Her cheeks flushed, which Paul thought quite endearing.

"As you can see, we're about to start practicing for next Sunday. Would you like to stay and listen?" He smiled, and didn't voice his next question. Or hang around to watch Adrian?

"No, I think I'd better go."

Adrian stepped forward to stand beside Celeste. "That's too bad. You'd probably be able to give us some constructive criticism." Adrian turned to Paul. "She wouldn't play anything for me, but you should see her electric grand."

Paul tried not to flinch when Randy's voice piped up behind him. He hadn't heard Randy coming, but now that Randy had discovered the action, anything could happen.

"Electric grand?" Randy asked. "You play? Are you any good?"

Celeste's face suddenly paled, which Paul thought odd.

"I'm okay," she muttered. "I really think I should go."

Randy blocked her path. "Wanna see my new electric piano? It's probably not as nice as yours, but it's got some really neat features."

Paul tried to bite back his grin. He never tired of watching Randy in action, especially around women.

Celeste looked doubtful. "But you're supposed to be practicing. I'm interrupting."

"You're not interrupting. We haven't started yet." Randy jerked his thumb over his shoulder. "It's in the other room."

Adrian cleared his throat and stepped forward. "Randy, didn't you hear the lady? She doesn't want to stay."

Randy covered his heart with his palms and turned, making direct eye contact with Celeste and Celeste only. "But I'm not very good. If you could give me some tips, I'd be forever in your debt."

Celeste's face flamed. Adrian's eyes narrowed.

Paul tried not to laugh. He was having more fun now than he would have if they had been practicing.

"Okay. I suppose I can at least look at it," Celeste mumbled. "Is it the same one you had at the church?"

Quietly, she followed Randy into Adrian's den, where everything was set up, ready to begin their practice.

Randy's new electric piano and Bob's drums sat in the back corner. The guitar amps were pushed against the wall. Paul's bass guitar lay in its case on the floor, as did Adrian's guitar.

Celeste played a few notes with one finger, reset a number of the effects buttons, and played a few chords.

"Yes, this is very nice. Now I think I'd better be going."

Randy shook his head so fast his hair flopped onto his forehead. "No. Wait." He fumbled with a handful of music and pulled out a song the group had been struggling with. "Can you play this for me? I'm not quite getting it. I'm not really good at this. I'd rather be working the sound system, but Paul said we needed someone on the keyboard."

Adrian cleared his throat. "Randy, will you move and let the woman go home?"

Randy batted his eyelashes at Celeste again. "Puh-lee-cccccze?"

"Uh… It's okay, Adrian. I guess…"

Randy turned to everyone else. "Can you guys play this one once, and I'll peek over Celeste's shoulder?"

Paul nodded. It was true that Randy wasn't very good on the keyboard, but he was all they had. Up until recently, they'd only used the guitars. When they'd added Randy on the keyboard, as poorly as Randy played, he'd filled a hole in the music they hadn't previously realized was there—when he wasn't fooling around and making mistakes.

Paul cleared his throat. "As long as she doesn't mind, and she's volunteering, I'm not going to refuse. Let's get started."

Bob parked himself behind the drums, and Paul and Adrian plugged in their guitars.

"Three, four!"

And they began to play.

They sounded better than they'd ever sounded in the entire time they'd played together.

After the last chord ended, silence permeated the room.

"I'll never play like that," Randy mumbled. "I quit."

Paul blinked a few times. "Did you say you were looking for a new church home? Were you on the worship team at your old church?"

Her face paled again. "No."

He waited for her to elaborate, but she didn't. He noticed Adrian didn't say anything, either.

Paul blinked again. "I can't believe this. You, Celeste, are the answer to our prayers."

Celeste remained silent.

Paul lowered his bass guitar into the stand. "If you can't tell, we really need you. The church needs you."

"But…"

Paul raised his palms to silence her protests. "I don't want to pressure you, but—"

"Oh, come on!" Adrian burst out. He stood between Paul and Celeste, his arms crossed over his chest. "You guys haven't left her alone from the moment she walked in the door! Talk about pressure. She's only just met you guys. And Randy, playing all your cute little tricks to get her sympathy. You all should be ashamed of yourselves."

"But…but…" Randy stammered, then turned to Celeste. "I think you can see the difference you made. You heard us on Sunday."

Paul watched the color drain from Celeste's cheeks as she and Randy faced off. "But what about you?" she asked.

"You're the one playing the keyboard. You're doing okay. Really. You are."

Randy cleared his throat and ran his fingers through his hair, an indication that for once, Randy was being serious. "Don't try to be nice. I listened to the tapes, so I know what I sound like. That's why I just quit, remember? My job is the sound system. That's what I like to do best. We need you on the piano."

Celeste stood staring at Randy with her mouth hanging open.

Paul turned his head to Bob, who had said nothing the entire time. One corner of Bob's mouth turned up, he glanced at Randy, and shrugged. "I think she sounded great, too." Bob turned to Celeste. "It's up to you, though."

Paul shook his head. "I know this is rather sudden for you. Tell you what. If you decide to take up residence with our little church, think about joining our worship team."

"But I've never been on a worship team before. I don't even know most of the songs."

"You did fine on the last one with no practice. I have a feeling *you* could be teaching *us*, even on the ones you supposedly don't know. Did your old church not do contemporary songs?"

"Actually, I haven't been going to church very long. That's why I don't know very many."

Paul knitted his brows as he tried to think. He'd been asking God for a long time to do something with their worship team. They weren't very good, but they were the best the church had.

He turned to study Celeste. On the previous Sunday he'd been surprised when Adrian hadn't sat with them during the morning service. Now he knew why. Because Paul wanted to see this person who had pulled his friend away, he was more than happy when they had all sat together for the evening service.

He shouldn't have, but he'd paid more attention to Celeste than he had to the pastor. She was obviously unfamiliar with the flow of the service, yet she showed a lot of enthusiasm over things Paul had long considered routine. She'd even taken notes when Pastor Ron was speaking, something Paul hadn't done for a long time. Watching her had been a sad reminder of how easily complacency crept in.

He told himself that was about to change.

"I know you're not sure, but I think it could work. We need you, and I think this is a good place for you to fit in, even though you're new. I'd really like it if we could all pray about it. Together. Right now."

She glanced back and forth between all the guys. "Well… I guess so."

Celeste followed the men into the living room, unable to believe what was happening. She did want to join their worship team. The strength of that realization took her breath away. Because she'd been working on becoming a professional musician, all God's music touched her.

But she hadn't been a Christian long enough to know about things like this. Not only was she a newcomer to this church, she was a newcomer to God's family. In addition to her new faith, everything in her life was in a state of flux. Because she tried to keep to herself, she wasn't even sure she was worshipping God properly. She had no one to ask if she was doing it right.

She doubted she was ready for the responsibility of being part of a team whose purpose was to lead others to praise and to worship God. Paul appeared to be a strong leader, so she would be under his tutelage, but she didn't know if that was enough.

Adrian and his friends sat on the couch and loveseat, leaving the easy chair for her.

Prior to praying with Adrian before they ate, and besides church, the only other time she'd prayed with someone else had been with her mother's neighbor, the woman who'd told her all about God. She'd never prayed in a small group.

All the men folded their hands in their laps.

"Let's pray," Paul said, and everyone bowed their heads.

The room fell silent. Celeste covered her face with her hands and bared her soul to God. She told Him how much being a part of their team would fill her empty heart, more than replacing what she had given up. She praised Him for the new friendships she could see, beginning with Adrian and his friends. She had liked them all immediately. And strangely enough, she trusted them as a group. Singly, that might be different, but when they were all together, she'd never felt more safe.

From her first step into Faith Community Fellowship, she'd experienced an instant peace. She knew she'd gone to the right place.

Adrian's voice broke the silence. *"Dear Heavenly Father. I pray for your guidance for Celeste as she makes her decision. I pray for your kindness and mercy upon her in this, and every area of her life. Thank you for your blessings and continued love, today, and forever."*

"Amen," Paul said softly.

Celeste sat straight, trying to maintain her composure. "Yes," she said, failing in her attempt to keep a tremor out of her voice. "I do want to be a part of this team. As long as it doesn't matter that I haven't been a Christian very long."

Paul smiled at her, his brown eyes sparkling with warmth. Just as with Adrian, she felt comfortable with him.

"That's great," Paul said. "The only thing we have to do is talk to Pastor Ron. And then he'll probably want to talk to you, too."

Celeste's heart went cold. "The pastor is going to want to talk to me?"

Paul nodded. "It will be just so he can get to know you a little, and, if I can be blunt, to know your heart is in the right place. It won't matter that you haven't been a Christian long. God doesn't have a trial waiting period. He takes you just as you are, just so long as your heart and soul are open to Him. And so will Pastor Ron."

Celeste forced herself to smile. She wasn't foolish enough to think just anyone who said they were a Christian and a good musician would be able to go up to the front and lead the congregation in worship. Pastor Ron would want to do more than just say hello. He would want to know about her, know something about her life before she walked in the door of his church.

She had fooled herself in thinking that if she didn't talk about it, it would go away. Now she would have to tell him everything, even though it was the last conversation she ever wanted to have.

Chapter Four

"Celeste? Not that I'm not happy to see you, but what are you doing here?"

Celeste gulped and looked up at Adrian, towering above her in the doorway. "I'm not sure. I just saw Pastor Ron. Maybe I should go home."

"Nonsense. Come in." Adrian pushed the door wide open, and stepped aside.

Celeste stepped into Adrian's living room, but her mind was still back in Pastor Ron's office.

She'd heard somewhere that confession was good for the soul. In some ways that was true, but now, not yet an hour later, she wondered if she'd done the right thing. It was Pastor Ron's job to forgive and accept her, regardless of what she'd done, whether or not she deserved it. However, she doubted the rest of God's flock would feel the same way, and that included Adrian and his friends.

Talking to Pastor Ron and telling him everything had been the hardest thing she'd ever done. Now that it was over, her first impulse was to go home and take something to calm her nerves, but that was one of the things she had put behind her. Still, she knew where to get anything she wanted, within minutes, no questions asked, as long as she had cash. It was easy, and no one would ever know.

Instead, she found herself at Adrian's house.

"So, how did it go?"

"Pastor Ron welcomed me to the church, and to the worship team. I don't know what to say."

Adrian's smile widened. "Don't be nervous, you'll be fine." He checked his wristwatch. "Have you had dinner? I was just about to throw a burger on the barbecue. I can easily make two."

She splayed her hands on her queasy stomach. "I don't know. I'm not sure how I feel. I don't even know why I'm here. I'm sorry to interrupt your dinner. I wasn't thinking."

"Don't be ridiculous." Adrian stepped back and extended one arm in the direction of his kitchen. "You're always invited. If you really don't want a burger, then the least I can do is offer you a cup of coffee."

Celeste followed him through the kitchen to his back patio, where his propane barbecue was heating up. He directed her to sit in one of the lawn chairs, then disappeared back into the kitchen. The microwave beeped while she waited. When he returned, he carried both a cup of coffee and a plate with two hamburger patties, both defrosted. As he placed both burgers on the grill, he peeked over his shoulder at her. "Just in case you change your mind."

Celeste's heart sped up to double time. If only she'd met someone like him eight years ago.

Adrian poked at the patties with his spatula. "I think I

speak for all of the guys when I say that I can hardly wait until Sunday when you'll be with us."

"You don't mean this Sunday? You mean next week, right?" She thought back to her previous experiences. Whenever she had performed without having practiced with the rest of the band, their audience had been too drunk to notice a few misplayed notes. This was different. Not only would everyone listening be thinking clearly, this was for God, and she wanted to do her best.

Completely serious, Adrian turned around. "I got an e-mail from Randy this afternoon, asking if I'd heard from you. He's already planned some new settings he's going to try. He fully intends to be in the sound room, not at the front, playing."

"I don't know if that's such a good idea."

Adrian shrugged his shoulders. "If it makes you feel any better, I phoned Paul after I read Randy's e-mail. He was really impressed with what you did yesterday. He's very excited about how we're going to sound with a *good* pianist. Frankly, we can't possibly be any worse. He said running through everything when we're setting up Sunday morning will be enough. But if you're nervous, I can go over the songs with you this evening. It's not the same, but it's better than nothing."

"I wanted to set my standards high. If you're willing to take the time, then I'd really appreciate it."

Adrian gave the burgers a flip. "Great. These are almost done. If you've hungry, come into the kitchen, and we can fix the buns. I left the other stuff inside because of the bugs."

A sudden breeze sent the aroma of the mouth-watering

burgers into her face. Her stomach grumbled. "That smells so good… But I don't know…"

Adrian turned down the heat, closed the lid of the barbecue, and escorted her into the kitchen to fix the buns. "I'd still be cooking and eating, even if you weren't here. Don't worry about it. It's no extra trouble."

It wasn't the trouble, or even the expense of feeding an extra person that caused Celeste to hesitate. This wasn't frozen supermarket pizza. It was a real dinner, and sharing dinner was too much like a date. She couldn't do that. The changes in her life were too new to be exploring such options, if she ever explored those options again. If she did, a nice man like Adrian wouldn't be interested in someone like her. Recounting the details of her life to Pastor Ron had served as a potent reminder of who she was, versus who she now appeared to be.

"I'd better not."

Adrian bunched up a towel and removed a tray of fries from the oven. "You don't want to make me eat all this by myself, do you?" He set the tray down and pressed his free hand to his very flat stomach.

"You'll never be fat," she mumbled.

"I'm not so sure, but there's only one way to save me from that fate, and that's to share so I don't eat it all myself. If you're in a rush, we could always eat while we practice."

She certainly didn't have anything else to do, but eating while they practiced was a way to make it work-related, which was good enough for her. "I think that's a great idea. Let's get set up."

All the instruments lay exactly as they'd been left the

day before. It felt strange playing without the rest of the band, but as promised, Adrian guided her through the songs to the best of his ability.

When they were done, Celeste clicked off the keyboard, then turned to Adrian. "You know, you're much better than you give yourself credit for. What you think is bad isn't lack of talent. It's just inexperience. It takes time to get good when you only practice together once a week. The dynamics are very different than when you're playing alone."

Adrian hesitated, then laid his guitar carefully into the case. "I appreciate you saying that. I've been working really hard at learning to play properly. These songs will sound even better than this on Sunday morning, when we'll all be together. Adding Bob on the drums makes a big difference."

Celeste hesitated. "I still don't think playing in front of the congregation without everyone having practiced together is a very good idea. This was good, but maybe we should wait until next week."

Adrian leaned down and turned off his amp. "Paul will be really disappointed if we don't play. Maybe I should e-mail everyone and ask if they're free for a short practice tomorrow evening."

Celeste gulped. "But tomorrow is Friday." Everyone she knew always had plans on Friday night. Big plans. But that was a different world. She didn't know what good, decent people did on Friday nights. Recently she had spent most nights alone in front of the television, but on Fridays, when the emptiness of her home haunted her, she went to the library. Even though she spent her time in solitude, there were other people around her, all quietly minding their own business. She'd even rediscovered the joy of reading, something she hadn't done for many years.

Adrian shrugged his shoulders. "I never talked to them about what they're doing, but they're probably free because none of us is seeing anyone right now. But I never thought to ask you first. I'm sorry. I should have realized. I can tell Paul we'll start playing together next week, after you can have a real practice on Wednesday with everyone."

Guilt roared through her. "It's certainly okay with me if it's okay with everyone else. I just thought you had plans."

He shook his head. "We've done last-minute stuff like this before, and it's always fun. I'll let you know what they say. Do you have an e-mail address? Or can I have your phone number?"

Her first impulse was to refuse, but she couldn't. She'd promised God that she would trust Adrian. Adrian already knew where she lived, and no more harm could be done if he had her phone number. However, the only e-mail address she had was at the office. By giving him the company name, he would know her last hiding place, where she worked, dissolving the last thread of the anonymity she'd worked so hard to achieve.

Before she changed her mind, Celeste scribbled her home phone number and e-mail address onto a scrap piece of paper. "Here they are. Now if you'll excuse me, it's getting late, and I should be getting home."

As usual, Celeste parked her mother's car where she figured it would be least noticeable, and hurried into the restaurant.

In midafternoon she'd received an e-mail from Adrian telling her that he'd finally heard back from everyone. No one had other plans, so they were going to practice as discussed, just a little earlier. Adrian had also hinted that he wanted to talk to her before everyone else got there, and so to be even earlier. Unfortunately she'd been asked to put in an hour of unplanned overtime, and now her stomach was growling. Since she didn't want Adrian to make supper for her again, and even though she really didn't have the money to spare, Celeste found herself at the fast-food restaurant a few blocks from home.

Celeste ordered the cheapest meal on the board and settled herself at a table, deliberately sitting with her back to the counter so no one entering the restaurant could see her face. She had just taken her first bite when a deep voice sounded behind her.

"Hi, Celeste. Mind if I join you? I saw your car, so I knew you were here."

Celeste choked, swallowed and recovered, but not in time to say anything as Randy lowered a full tray of food onto her table. He parked himself in the opposite chair and smiled a greeting. "This is great. It's nice not to eat alone."

Celeste pressed her fist into the center of her chest and cleared her throat. Unlike Randy, she had wanted to eat alone. Still, she considered Randy to be safe. This was okay, but she hoped that no one else she knew would associate her with her mother's car. "Hi, Randy. It's good to see you." Strangely, as soon as the words were said, she found she meant them.

Randy bowed his head briefly as he took time out to pray over his food in silence, then removed the wrapper from his burger. "I think I know where you're going after you eat." He paused and grinned. "And speaking of Adrian, when—"

"Hi, Celeste," a male voice called out from behind them, cutting off Randy's words.

Celeste's heart pounded. She turned her head so quickly her neck hurt.

As she raised her hand to rub the sore muscle, Bob approached, also carrying a tray brimming with junk food. "I saw your car in the lot." Bob's eyes moved slightly as he glanced at Randy, then back to her. His smile flickered, then resumed. "Hi, Randy," he muttered, his voice not as cheerful as it had been in his greeting to Celeste. He lowered his tray to the table.

Celeste didn't see it, but she heard the double thump of Randy's feet landing on the chair where Bob obviously intended to sit. With Randy's feet taking up the third chair, Randy deposited an empty bag on the fourth chair. He leaned back, raised his arms, and linked his fingers behind his head. "Sorry. All the chairs at this table are taken." He released his hands from behind his head, shoveled a few fries into his mouth, then resumed his position, grinning while he chewed.

"Grow up, Randy," Bob grumbled, unceremoniously pulling the chair out from underneath Randy's feet. Randy's feet landed on the floor with a thump. Bob brushed any potential dirt off the seat with his fingers, then sat. "I think I know where you two are going."

She forced herself to smile. "Yes. I know where you're going, too."

Bob closed his eyes and bowed his head slightly for a couple of seconds, then unwrapped his burger and dumped the cardboard envelope of fries onto the corner of the wrapper. "It's nice to see you here, although I kind of expected Adrian would be with you, not Randy."

Randy's grin widened. "Sometimes the best man really does win."

Bob rolled his eyes, then pointedly faced Celeste. "Speaking of Adrian, I guess—"

Another male voice broke through Bob's words. "Hi, Celeste!" Paul lowered only the corner of his tray to the table, because the surface didn't have enough room for it. "I saw your car in the lot."

Celeste didn't know why this time she wasn't surprised.

Paul emptied a burger, fries and a drink onto the table, then set the tray on the empty table beside them. He hesitated for a second when he saw the empty bag on the last chair. He picked it up, shook it to confirm it was empty, dropped it on the tray at the other table, and sat. "Hi, Randy. Bob," he said as he quickly acknowledged his friends. He paused to bow his head slightly, closed his eyes for a second, then began to unwrap his burger. "This is funny. The only one missing is Adrian."

In unison, Bob and Randy turned their heads toward the door, as if thinking about him would make Adrian appear.

When he didn't, they turned back to Paul.

Paul turned to Celeste. "Are you ready for our first practice together?"

Celeste nodded. "I've been thinking about it all day. I'm really looking forward to it, but Adrian might not be. This will be his third time practicing the same selection of songs in as many days. I hope he doesn't find it too boring."

Randy snickered. "We're talking about Adrian, aren't we?"

The other two snickered as well. Celeste didn't know what was so funny.

Paul's grin straightened. "We should probably explain. Because he's an accountant, we tease Adrian constantly about his boring job. Repetition doesn't bother him. It's just the way he is. But I guess you already know that."

"Actually, I haven't known Adrian very long." Yet, in that short time, she couldn't help but like him. She wanted to get to know him better, but at the same time, the thought scared her to death.

Paul set his burger down and began to nibble on his fries. "I wonder if seeing you playing the piano reminds Adrian of when he was a kid. He took lessons for a while when we were in elementary school. That was one thing he could never master. Usually kids quit on their own, but Adrian wouldn't give up. He just kept plugging along until finally his mother couldn't stand it anymore and suggested that he try something else."

"Adrian told me that you all grew up together, right here in this neighborhood."

Randy nodded. "Yeah. We've been friends since we were kids. Through thick and thin. We watch out for each other, but especially for Adrian." Randy paused, and his voice lowered. "Sometimes people tend to take advantage of him."

Celeste swirled a fry in a blob of ketchup. She could certainly understand how that could happen. He'd been helpful to her in so many ways. Everything his friends said about Adrian confirmed that he was as good a man as her heart told her he was. She also had no doubt that he really did call his mother as often as his phone bill indicated.

He'd even arranged an extra practice, just for her on Friday night, when everyone else should have had other, more interesting things to do. "I know what you mean. I feel like I'm taking advantage of him already."

All movement at their table stopped. Without looking, she knew they were all watching her. She refused to make eye contact. Instead, she began concentrating intently on the blob of ketchup, not raising her head as she spoke. "I mean with the worship team, and the extra practice. He's also offered to help me get acquainted with the neighborhood."

A silence hung in the air. Bob was the first to speak. "That's right. I remember now. That's why he was late on Wednesday. You'd been shopping together. Adrian said he forgot we moved the practice to an earlier time than usual, which was really strange. It's a good thing Paul has a key."

A wave of guilt passed through her. She'd felt bad enough about making Adrian late, but Bob's reminder made her feel even worse. "I'm really sorry about that. He never said he had plans."

Bob smiled gently. "Don't worry about it. If he hadn't forgotten his stuff, then you wouldn't have come over, and we never would have known that you play piano. And quite well, too. I've always believed in God's timing."

She still wasn't so sure of the timing being from God. Being able to play well didn't seem to be the major criterion for being on their team. Still, the timing was good because she now had the opportunity to use her talents to serve God, which was infinitely better than what she was doing with them before.

Bob clasped his hands, rested them on the table, and leaned forward. "After you left the other night we asked

Adrian about you, and he had so many good things to say. I was wondering if you two were an item or something. It's not often he talks about a woman, especially someone none of us already know. I can't help but be curious about you."

"No," she said quickly, trying to keep her voice calm. "We're not an 'item'. We're just…" Her voice trailed off as she tried to think of how to describe her relationship with Adrian. They certainly weren't dating. She couldn't call him a friend. She didn't have any friends any more and she hadn't known Adrian long enough to call him a new friend. He was really little more than a stranger.

At best, if she had to put a label on it, they were only casual acquaintances. But she couldn't say that to Bob, Randy and Paul.

"We're just…" She forced herself to smile, hoping Bob wouldn't misunderstand. "…getting to know each other better. Since we're almost neighbors, and all that."

One eyebrow quirked. "I see. I was just curious. If you don't mind me asking, I was wondering if there's anyone else who would mind that you're, uh, getting to know Adrian better. I noticed you came to church alone."

Celeste blinked. She wondered if Adrian had been hurt by a woman recently, and that was why his friends were acting this way. Their obvious concern served as another reminder of the absence of such friends in her life. When she needed help, no one stood up for her. She'd been all but abandoned.

She'd never needed a friend more in her life than right now. She wanted to have these four men as friends, but she couldn't ask or expect such a thing because it would be too one-sided. They freely gave their time, energy and dedication to each other. She had nothing to offer but trouble, bad examples and poor judgment.

But as to Bob's question, she didn't know how to answer. There was definitely someone who would mind, even though what she did and who she saw were no longer any of Zac's business. She'd told him she would leave unless he had a change of heart, since their priorities had become so vastly different. Zac had only laughed at her, so she'd done exactly what she'd said she was going to do. It shouldn't have been a surprise, but she knew that Zac would have been very, very angry when he discovered that she was gone.

If she continued on in the way she was doing, Zac would never find her, and he would never know what she did or who she spent her time with. Therefore, technically, at least, there was no one who could mind that she was getting to know Adrian better.

"Actually, I recently broke up with someone. It was a bad situation, and I'm glad it's over," she said abruptly. "I'm looking forward to a new start." They didn't know how much of a new start it really was, and she had no intention of telling them any of the details. She ached with the need to have them respect her, even though she didn't deserve it.

Paul set his drink down on the table, and folded his hands. "All of us are pretty settled. Then if you don't have ties elsewhere, do you think you'll settle here at our little church or do you tend to move around a lot?"

Celeste forced herself to breathe. She honestly didn't know. Too much depended on circumstances beyond her control, and how much she could keep to herself. "My new job is close by, so that's the main reason I decided to move here." She tried her best to smile and left her thoughts unsaid.

Paul grew serious, and didn't reply immediately. She suspected he was considering her in connection with their discussion of roots. She had no roots. Even the car they acknowledged as hers wasn't her own; it was borrowed. She didn't even know when her mother would return so they could trade back.

"I knew that you had only been to our church a couple of times, so I find it unusual that Adrian pushed so much for you to be on the worship team without knowing you really well first. It's not like Adrian to do anything…impulsive." One eye narrowed slightly as he continued to watch her.

Celeste felt like a bug under a microscope. She felt as if she was being interviewed, to be sure she was worthy of their friend.

A knot formed in her stomach. Adrian was solid and stable, the exact opposite of her with her new job, her recent move, her new church and her complete lack of anyone she could call a friend, regardless of what she was trying to do with her life. She wasn't ready to tell them what she was trying to put behind her. It had been hard enough to tell the pastor, whose job it was to keep sensitive issues confidential.

The truth was that if she wanted to take advantage of Adrian, she knew all the tricks. If Adrian was as innocent and trusting as his friends indicated, he would be an easy mark—his friends were right to think Adrian needed protection from her. If she wanted to, she could taint him simply by being a bad influence, just as Zac had eventually tainted her. She wasn't going to do that to Adrian. One ruined life was enough.

The words of their pastor, *her* pastor now, echoed in Celeste's head. He'd even helped her memorize the reference from Corinthians.

Therefore, if anyone is in Christ, he is a new creation; the old has gone, the new has come.

As of three weeks, two days and seven hours ago, she was a new creation. The old Celeste was gone. The new Celeste was on the worship team, where she would be serving the God who had loved her before she loved Him. Even though it was Friday night, she found she now wanted to do 'church stuff' when everyone else was out partying.

"Impulsive or not, I'm really grateful for the opportunity to settle into a nice church so quickly. It's something I really need to do."

Paul blinked, and his smile resumed. "And impulsive or not, we really needed a good pianist. A strong female voice from the front is a definite bonus, too. I'm glad we've all come together like this. Now let's go, before Adrian starts to worry."

Chapter Five

Adrian struggled not to pace.

They were late. All of them.

He could see Randy being late. Maybe Paul. But never Bob.

He peeked through the blinds, then strode into the kitchen to check the coffee for the tenth time.

He didn't know if Celeste was habitually late, or if he should worry about her. What he did know was that she had told him she would try to be early. Not only was she not early, she was late. She hadn't even phoned, despite the fact that he'd helped her program his number into her new cellular phone.

Adrian returned to the living room and peeked through the blinds again. Her earlier assurances that the car ran fine once it started did nothing to convince him it was mechanically sound. He'd heard the way it chugged. Fortunately, her e-mail address showed the name of the company where she worked. If he couldn't reach her via her cell phone, it would be a simple matter to retrace her route with his car.

He let the slats slip from between his fingers. He didn't remember praying for patience recently, but if he had, he was receiving a very ironic lesson.

He walked to the CD player, where he selected some music to pass the time and to occupy his mind while he waited.

Celeste was getting to him.

She was different from anyone he'd ever met, yet he couldn't pinpoint what he found so fascinating about her.

She appeared ambitious because she'd talked of signing up for night-school classes while working full-time. She'd also mentioned a part-time second job she'd recently quit. She hadn't told him exactly what it was, only that it involved a partnership that was now dissolved. Yet, for someone who appeared eager to get ahead and not afraid of hard work, she only held an entry level position, and her apartment held nothing of any value except for her piano.

Because the car she was driving belonged to her mother, he didn't know exactly what kind of vehicle she did own, or its age or condition. She'd only told him it was an economy import. Therefore, he doubted she spent all her money on her car. Neither did she spend her money on clothes or other women's accessories. Every time he'd seen her she'd been well-dressed, but nothing she wore was spectacular or even particularly trendy, merely practical. She didn't spend all her money on vacations—she'd told him she had never been out of the country.

She didn't even own her home, she rented.

He closed his eyes and said a quick prayer that she didn't spend all her money on medical expenses, then returned to the kitchen.

Just as Adrian reached for the phone, a rumble reverberated from outside. It became louder, suddenly stopped, then was immediately followed by an uneven series of clunks and chugs before becoming completely silent.

Adrian smiled. Celeste had arrived.

As he walked through the living room the noise of another car arriving echoed from outside. It stopped, and a door closed. Then another and another.

Adrian opened the door to see Celeste approaching, with Bob, Paul and Randy close behind.

Celeste walked up the steps, carrying a drink from the local fast-food restaurant. "I had really planned to be here sooner. Sorry. I don't know where the time went."

Adrian's smile dropped as he saw his three friends carrying paper cups with the same logo. He saw where the time had gone, and it wasn't with him.

He cleared his throat and forced himself to smile politely, trying to hide his hurt feelings at not being invited. "That's okay. You're here now." He paused just long enough for his three friends to file past him into the living room. "In fact, it's funny that you all arrived at exactly the same time."

Randy grinned and held up his drink. "Yeah. We all saw Celeste's car at the restaurant as we were driving by, and then we all decided to go in, one at a time. Isn't that funny?"

"Yeah. Hilarious."

Randy sipped his drink, which only resulted in a loud, echoing sound at the bottom of the cup. "I hope you bought donuts. We were so busy talking, we didn't have time for dessert."

"Yes. I stopped on the way home."

Everyone else filed into the den, but Randy turned and headed for the kitchen.

Soon Randy joined them, donut in hand, and made his adjustments in the sound system. The practice progressed well, and when they were finished, Adrian was even more impressed with Celeste than he had been when the two of them had practiced together without the benefit of the other instruments.

His opinion was confirmed by Paul, who was grinning ear to ear when he laid his bass guitar into the case. "Your other church's loss is definitely our gain. I think the rest of the congregation is going to feel the same way Sunday morning."

Her cheeks darkened as she looked up at Paul. "In some ways, I'm looking forward to it, and in other ways I'm scared to death."

At her hesitant smile, Adrian's heart went out to her. He would never forget the first time he and his friends had been up at the front of the church. He'd never admitted it to anyone, but he'd been scared, too. Unlike Celeste, however, he wasn't very good, and he knew it. Now, four months later, he and his friends had obtained a measure of proficiency, but it had taken a lot of practice, and there was still plenty of room for improvement.

He cleared his throat as he lowered his own guitar into the case. "You'll be fine once everything gets started. Just remember what you're there for, and that the congregation is there for the same reason, which is to worship God."

She nodded. "Yes, of course. I'll remember that."

Randy checked his watch. "If you don't mind, I'm going

to go home. Tomorrow is my regular weekly meeting. First we're doing breakfast, and then it's my turn to say a few words. We've got a couple of newcomers, so that's really important. Then we have an early tee time."

Celeste turned the piano off. "Tee time? I wish my boss included tee time in our meetings."

Randy shrugged his shoulders. "It's not that kind of meeting. This is something I never miss. Maybe I'll tell you about it someday."

Adrian nodded. "I know the right words will come to you. See you Sunday morning."

Instead of going through the living room, Randy detoured through the kitchen before Adrian heard the front door open and close.

Bob began to pack up the drums. Paul helped tuck the cymbals into their totes. "I've got to go soon, too," said Bob. "Bart is taking the day off tomorrow, so I've got to get up early to go open up." He turned to Celeste. "A 7:00 a.m. opening makes for a very short Friday night."

Paul lifted one of the toms from the drum stand. "Then go. I'll finish this."

"Great. I appreciate it. See you Sunday."

Bob also left, but he went straight through the living room on his path to the front door.

Adrian's heart raced. With both Randy and Bob gone, he secretly willed Paul to leave also, even though he knew he wasn't being very gracious.

Paul smiled. "Then I guess it's just the three of us left to finish off the donuts. Depending on how many Randy already ate."

Adrian tried to control his disappointment that Paul was

staying. Not that he really cared about the donuts. He'd only been hoping for some time alone with Celeste. He wanted to get to know her better, and that meant talking to her without Paul being there. He'd already seen that it was hard for Celeste to open up, especially in a group setting. Then, when she did, she focused on exactly what she'd been asked, and nothing more.

Adrian could understand that Celeste didn't like to talk about herself. Despite his recent tendency to talk too much, he usually didn't talk about himself, either. But Celeste's almost deliberate omissions when someone asked her a question only served to make him more curious than ever.

He glanced toward the kitchen as he thought of how he could discourage Paul from staying. "I don't know how much coffee is left. I think Randy finished it off along with the donuts."

Celeste moved from the piano and began to help Paul disassemble the drums. "Let me help, and it will go faster," she said as she lifted the snare and released the tension clip for the coil underneath. It tweaked Adrian's interest that she knew to do that.

"I should probably be going, too, soon as I'm done here," she said as she began taking the high-hat cymbal apart, without the need for instruction.

Adrian folded down the guitar stands and music stands, and stacked them at the side of the room. "I'd love for you to stay and have a cup of tea." He lowered his voice just a bit. "When I was out buying the donuts, I also picked up some of the same herbal tea I saw in your grocery cart the other day."

Both eyebrows raised and she said, "Really? You did that for me?"

He didn't understand her surprise. It was just a box of tea. All he could do was nod.

"In that case, I'd love to stay for a while. As long I won't be keeping you from anything."

Adrian checked his watch. "It's already ten o'clock, so it's a little late to be starting something. Unless you have to get up early in the morning, too?"

"No. I'm fine."

When they were done, the three of them retired to the kitchen. Adrian put a mug of water in the microwave for Celeste's tea, while Paul walked straight for the coffeepot.

"There's still some left. Just enough for two cups, which is perfect, since Celeste is having tea," Paul said as he divided the last of the coffee.

Adrian pushed the buttons on the microwave. "What are you doing tomorrow?"

"I've got to start thinking ahead for school and look over my lesson plans for the coming year," Paul said as he poured some cream into his coffee. "There's only a couple of weeks left of summer, and I don't want to leave it too late."

Adrian turned to his friend. "I didn't mean you. I already know what you're doing. I was talking to Celeste."

Paul only laughed.

Adrian turned back to Celeste. "So, Celeste. What are you doing tomorrow?"

Celeste smiled. "Nothing, really. I'll probably just sit in the backyard and read. I picked up a new book on my way home from work yesterday."

Adrian handed her the mug and the box for the tea so she could select her own teabag. "That sounds like a nice way to spend a hot summer afternoon. I've got a pile of reading to catch up on, including something that's due back at the library in a few days that I haven't even started. Why don't I join you, and we can share a pitcher of lemonade?"

Behind him, Paul muffled a groan. Adrian wanted to kick him. Instead, he spun around and glared at his friend. "Are you sure you don't have someplace else to go?"

Paul grinned. "Nope. I wouldn't miss this for anything in the world."

Celeste had started to dunk a teabag into the water. For an almost indiscernible moment, her movement stopped. "I'm sorry, Adrian, I don't know if that's such a good idea."

Adrian turned back to Celeste and tried to pretend he was interested in selecting a donut out of the box. "Why not? I'm not doing anything, either. So if both of us are doing nothing, we might as well do nothing together."

"Uh…"

"Don't you think that makes sense? Then later, maybe I can take you on a walking tour of the neighborhood as the day cools down. I sit far too much during the week, so I try to get out on the weekends. I've considered getting a dog, but I don't know if it's fair to keep an animal locked up inside while I'm gone to work all day."

Paul snorted under his breath, then began to laugh. "Are you comparing Celeste to a dog?"

"That does it. You've just overstayed your welcome."

Of course Paul didn't move, but Adrian hoped that Paul would at least take the hint. He usually tolerated Paul's 'input' into his love life, not that he had much, if any love life. But this time, he not only didn't think Paul was being very funny, Adrian didn't appreciate Paul's interference, in jest or otherwise.

Adrian stiffened, straightened his glasses, and turned around, ready to tell Paul that for once, he could mind his own business. The second they made eye contact, Paul's demeanor changed. Paul's smile dropped, his eyes widened, he quickly glanced at Celeste, then focused back on Adrian's face.

"Sorry," Paul mumbled. "I think I'm getting punchy after such a great practice." He stood, grabbing the last donut and one of the mugs on his way up. "Speaking of practice, I can't find my tuning meter. I think I forgot it here on Wednesday."

Without another word, Paul disappeared from the kitchen.

Adrian smiled, hoping he could still salvage some small fragments of his dignity. "Now that he's gone, at least temporarily, what do you think about getting together tomorrow afternoon? Nothing formal. If it turns into dinner, fine, but if not, that's fine, too. I'll understand if you already have other plans for later."

He waited for her response, knowing he was wearing his heart on his sleeve, opening himself up for her to tear it to shreds.

"I don't know. I have a lot of stuff to think about. But I guess it wouldn't hurt to sit in the same backyard and share some sunshine. Sure. Just so long as you don't mind if Hank and his wife, my landlords, are also outside on their side of the yard."

Adrian took that to mean they were meeting on her turf, which was fine with him. "That sounds good."

"I still owe you a dinner, so how about if I make us something for lunch?"

"I didn't feed you yesterday expecting the favor would be returned, but I'm never going to turn down a free home-cooked meal. You're on."

Before he could offer to bring fresh donuts, Paul returned. The conversation turned to idle chatter, which was fine with Adrian.

Tomorrow was another day, and tomorrow he would have Celeste all to himself.

Celeste tried to concentrate, but the words were without meaning. She'd never had a problem reading before, unless she'd taken something she knew would impair her thought processes. But at those times, intellectual pursuits had been the furthest thing from her mind.

She tucked in a bookmark, and set the book on the table. "I think I'm going to go into the house for more lemonade. How are you doing?"

Without looking at her, Adrian picked up his glass, swirled it, then set it back down on the table, all the while keeping his attention totally focused on his book. "I'm fine. Thanks."

She waited for him to say more, but he didn't. In fact, since lunch, when they had retired to the backyard and both had begun to read, she could have counted all the words he'd said on her fingers without reusing any of them.

She didn't know if she should have been insulted at his silence, or relieved. He hadn't told her everything she'd done wrong at the practice. He hadn't sat back and told her to fetch him a snack. He wasn't even trying to engage her in conversation. In the quiet setting of the backyard, there was no need for words or even music to fill the empty air. He was completely comfortable with the day, and with her. He'd said he'd come over for the afternoon to read, and that was exactly what he was doing.

Not only was Adrian reading, he was fully engrossed in the story. A few times he smiled, and once she even heard a small chuckle. Yet, he didn't stop or make any movements that would break the flow of his reading, other than occasionally straightening his glasses. The movement gave him an aura of being intellectual, but realistically, wearing glasses only meant he didn't have twenty/twenty vision. Yet, between the plain, clean style of his glasses, his good posture, and his trendy polo shirt with matching shorts, she found the overall picture of Adrian Braithwaite fascinating.

She couldn't believe she'd found a man like Adrian. The only thing she could see about him that wasn't perfect was that he talked too much when he was nervous, and he became rather impatient when things didn't run on his time-line. But those things she didn't mind, at least not too much.

Adrian's friends had joked about him being so predictable, but Celeste saw him from a different perspective. She knew many predictable people—people she could predict would do what was best for themselves, regardless of the cost to others.

Adrian wasn't merely predictable. Everyone could depend on Adrian to be honorable—in all the ways that counted.

Despite the fact that she hadn't known him long, she knew he would be an easy man to love. Of course, that he was tall, dark, handsome and had great legs was an added bonus.

Celeste almost pinched herself to bring herself back to reality. For the first time since she could remember, she felt happy, content and safe. Just as Pastor Ron had told her, her life was changing as her priorities were changing, just as God had promised when He made her a new creation. Every new and good thing in her life was tangible proof that God really was a god of mercy, and that miracles really did happen.

Before Adrian noticed she'd been studying him, Celeste stood and returned to the kitchen to refill her glass. While she did so, visions of a new life cascaded through her head, as strong as a rushing torrent. Things she wanted, but didn't think she could ever have until recently. A house of her own, just like the one in which she now lived. A little fluffy dog, just like the one a few doors down—a dog who wagged his tail and hopped around until she patted him, not an untrained pit bull that she was always afraid of.

And a man who loved her as much as she loved him.

"Celeste? Are you in here?"

Celeste fumbled with her glass, barely righting it before she spilled it. She pressed one hand to her chest. "You scared me. I didn't hear you come in."

"I was wondering why you were taking so long." He glanced at the now-empty pitcher.

She looked up into his warm hazel eyes, unable to speak. If the same situation had happened with Zac, by now Zac would either be demanding that she fix him something to eat, or groping her. Fool that she had been, she would have complied.

"I was going to make more lemonade. I guess I got distracted."

He stood to the side while she began to measure the mix into the pitcher. When she dumped in the second scoop, a poof of powder wafted up. She sneezed, causing her to spill the third scoop on the counter.

"Oops," she muttered, mentally kicking herself that she couldn't even make lemonade with Adrian watching her. She wet the dishcloth and was half way through wiping it up when the phone rang.

"Can you get that? My hands are all sticky."

Adrian picked up the phone and greeted the caller. His brows knitted, and he listened. After a few seconds he flinched, then finally spoke. "Who is this?"

Celeste could hear the caller's laugh from where she stood.

Without saying goodbye, Adrian hung up the phone. "It's a good thing you didn't answer that," he mumbled. "It was an obscene phone call. And it was really obscene."

Celeste froze. Unless she was mistaken, she'd heard that laugh before.

Fear coursed through her veins, turning her insides to ice.

She cleared her throat and forced herself to speak, hoping her voice sounded more natural than it felt. "I don't suppose he said his name."

"Of course not. But it was really strange. The first thing he said was your phone number, which is why I didn't hang up. Most of the time obscene calls are random dialing. I also found it strange than he didn't hang up when a male voice answered, but I can't even begin to imagine what goes on in the mind of a person who does stuff like that. I'm guessing he just paged through the phone book, put his finger on a number and dialed. You haven't had any other similar calls, have you?"

"No." She could see someone doing what Adrian suggested, but the main trouble with Adrian's theory was that she wasn't listed in the directory. She'd paid to have an unlisted phone number. The only people to whom she'd given her home number were her mother, the lady who lived next door to her mother, Adrian and Pastor Ron. She hadn't even given her landlord her phone number, because Hank lived right next door in the duplex and she hadn't had the new number when she filled out the forms.

Only two men had the number, or at least two men she could account for.

Adrian was with her. She doubted Pastor Ron would have made such a call.

"Celeste? Are you okay? You look pale."

She shrugged her shoulders, then quickly walked to the sink and began to wash her hands, using it as opportunity to turn her face away so she wouldn't have to lie. She was far from okay. If the caller was who she thought he was, it was her worst nightmare come true. It would mean her past had caught up with her.

But that couldn't be happening. She had an unlisted phone number. She had a new home and a new job here in Appleton, far away from her old stomping grounds. She hadn't been in contact with a single person she'd known before. She didn't even have her own car.

She told herself it was simply a random prank; some sicko had written down the phone number before he dialed, just to frighten his victim.

It worked. She was frightened, but she repeated over and over in her mind that the worst thing to have happened couldn't have happened.

If Zac knew where she now lived, he wouldn't have phoned. He would have appeared in person to let her know what he thought of what she'd done, both to him and the band, then make her take the consequences as he deemed fit.

If that happened, she would need more than a hiding place. She would need an army to protect her.

Even if she didn't need protection right that moment, good sense dictated that she tell someone the possibilities, so if something happened, someone would know the reason, and who to look for.

But it was just a phone call. Zac hadn't appeared at her door.

But she could see Zac spouting off to a man who answered, to make the fear worse, to tell more than one person that he was there, as a form of torture.

But Zac wouldn't be content just with a phone call. If it were Zac, Zac would do his torturing in person.

It couldn't have been Zac.

It was a random prank.

She was still safe.

As soon as her heart stopped pounding, Celeste turned around.

"I was a little shaken up, but I'm fine now. Do you want to go back outside?"

Adrian grinned from ear to ear. "Yeah. I'm finding it hard to put that book down, which is bad because I have to get up early for church tomorrow. By the way, since we're aiming to arrive at the same time, would you like me to pick you up?"

"Yes, I'd like that." The second the words were out of her mouth, Celeste nibbled on her bottom lip. Her acceptance of Adrian's offer wasn't from fear. She was accepting the ride because on Sunday morning her neighbors liked to sleep in, the car would make too much noise early in the morning.

She picked up the glass. "Let's get back to reading. I was just getting to a good part, too."

Just as he'd predicted, it was late by the time Adrian turned the last page of the book. They both yawned as she saw him to the door.

Adrian tucked the book under his arm. "I meant it when I said I should take you on a walking tour of the neighborhood. In fact, that might be a good idea tomorrow afternoon, between church services."

Celeste stilled, her hand on the doorknob. One of the reasons she had accepted his invitation so quickly was that she had the feeling his friends would tag along to talk about their first Sunday morning together.

But to spend an afternoon walking around opened up a whole new realm of possibilities. His friends wouldn't be joining them for a walk. There would be no books, no music, no distractions, and nothing else to do except talk. Between points of interest, it would be natural, even expected, to keep talking of personal things. Now, more than ever, she didn't want him to know anything about her life prior to the last three weeks. However, Adrian had already volunteered so much information about himself that it wasn't fair not to tell him anything in return.

She looked up at him while he waited patiently for her to reply. She didn't know yet how much she could tell him, but she had to tell him something.

She forced herself to smile, and hoped it didn't look as phony as it felt. "Sure. we can do that. Goodnight, Adrian."

She noticed that he'd come without his car.

As he walked away, Celeste watched until he turned the corner and disappeared.

If she didn't mess up what God had given her, she could be happy here, especially with a friend like Adrian.

If… she shuddered at the thought… she didn't have to tell him more than he needed to know. Then, they could stay 'friends.'

Chapter Six

"And that's where Mr. and Mrs. McHenry live. They're that elderly couple who yelled out 'Amen' at the close of the last song before the sermon."

"I remember them. I talked to them after the service. They're really nice."

Celeste smiled, which made Adrian smile, too. He'd been pleased with the way the congregation had welcomed Celeste into their midst, which was especially a relief to him because of the short amount of time she'd been attending. Most of the people there had never met her before, yet suddenly, she'd appeared at the front with Adrian and his friends, as if she belonged there.

He couldn't keep his smile from growing bigger, so he turned away.

She did belong there. He'd stood beside her while they played. He couldn't think of any other way to describe her other than to say that she was a natural in front of people. She might have been nervous at the practice, but once in front of the congregation, she suddenly relaxed, and even smiled and waved at one of the teen boys who obviously was trying to impress his friends that he could connect with the hot new chick at the front. She'd not only charmed the group of boys, but Adrian couldn't help but be impressed with her graciousness.

Celeste had interacted well with everyone she'd met from the congregation, and she was the perfect addition to their worship team. Without her there, their mistakes created gaps which interrupted the flow of worship—people didn't know what to do for the seconds it took the team to recover. Celeste completely filled out the sound, and covered magnificently whenever anyone else made a mistake. This morning, everything had been as close to perfect as it could possibly be.

Paul was right. Having Celeste join them truly was the answer to their prayers. She was probably even the answer to the prayers of many people in the congregation.

He wondered if Celeste was also the answer to his personal prayers.

As much as he'd enjoyed the book yesterday, plus the fact the he'd been able to drop it off at the library without having to pay an overdue fine before he finished it, the day had been somewhat of a test for Celeste.

He already knew she didn't chatter incessantly, a trait he hated and saw far too much in women, especially when they saw him as husband material.

Celeste had been perfectly content to read her book. He noticed she was a bit distracted at first, but he assumed that was probably because neither of them were talking. Once she became accustomed to his silence while he read, she relaxed and enjoyed her book too. Once they passed that stage, the day had been comfortable, even refreshing. They each knew the other was there, and that they could enjoy the day together without the need for constant conversation.

Of course, unless they talked, he wasn't going to get to know her better, which, for now, was his primary objective.

He pointed to his right. "A block that way is the community center, playground and a small park, where we all spent a lot of time as kids." He smiled with the memories of the good times he'd had in the park with his friends. "Did you go to the park when you were a kid?"

"Yes. I actually used to spend a lot of time as a kid playing catch with my dad. I have to admit that I think he really wanted a son. I was quite good at baseball, but when he died I quit the team. It wasn't the same without him there, and playing without him cheering for me was too much of a reminder that he was gone."

He remembered Celeste commenting about her mother, but this was the first time she'd said anything about her father. Now he knew. "I'm sorry. How old were you when he died?"

She sighed. "I was thirteen. He died in a construction accident when a scaffolding collapsed. He'd just gotten that big car. It wasn't new or anything, but it was his pride and joy. That's why my mom has kept it all these years."

A vision of the aging monstrosity flashed through his mind. Doing a little mental math, the car wasn't new when her father first bought it, and confirmed his impression that her family didn't have much money, even back then.

"Maybe us guys can get together and do something with it before your mother comes back. How long is she away for?"

"She just retired, and to celebrate not having to go back to work anymore, she took off to visit her sister. She says she'll be back when my aunt gets sick of looking at her, or refuses to feed her anymore."

Doing a little more mental math, Adrian calculated that Celeste was born later in her parents' lives. He already knew she was an only child, unlike himself, the youngest of four boys.

What he really wanted to know was, if her mother had planned the trip well in advance, why had Celeste chosen to rent the duplex instead of simply living at her mother's house?

"If your mother isn't there, and you're here, then who is looking after things? I mean mowing the grass, taking in the mail and stuff like that. I couldn't help but notice that you haven't been going back and forth to check on things."

"A neighbor, who is also my mother's best friend, is doing all that stuff. She's also the same lady who helped me find the duplex I'm renting. She knows Hank. She's the one who told me about Jesus."

Things were getting curiouser and curiouser. For every answer she gave him, she created ten more new questions.

"I'm always interested to hear how my friends came to find Jesus. Especially if they did as adults. I know you haven't been a Christian for very long."

Her step hesitated, but she kept moving. When she spoke, she kept her face directly forward, not looking at him. "There's not much to tell. I was having a rough time in my life with a lot of things. I felt as though everyone was taking advantage of me, and then, when I needed someone to stand up for me, no one would—except my mother's neighbor. She let me stay at her summer cottage for a few days, where it was just her and me. She told me that because of Jesus, someone once did something similar for her, so she wanted to do the same for me while I got my head together. She refused to accept anything from me. She wouldn't even take money to pay for the groceries I ate. She told me how much Jesus loved me, and that Jesus would help me do the right thing. He did, and here I am."

Adrian waited for her to say more, but she didn't. Contrary to her claim that there wasn't much to tell, he suspected there was a lot more, because instead of sounding triumphant, she sounded defeated, which wasn't the way it was supposed to be.

His heart went out to her. He wished he could take the sadness out of her voice and convince her that whatever her heartaches were, they were in the past. Jesus was her future, and because of Jesus, she could have friends and a real community here, in his neighborhood, with him, to be there for her when she needed someone. Starting with himself.

Since she was feeling alone, Adrian figured that a little knowledge would help bring her closer to feeling that she could be a part of the community. After all, that was what their walking tour was about in the first place.

"If you want to have a little history, here's Woo's Market. It's a typical family corner-store business, now owned by the third generation of Woos. Paul, Bob, Randy and I went to school with Charlie Woo, and he's now running the place with his wife Jolie. Let's stop and buy you a drink. My treat. I don't know about you, but I'm getting thirsty."

She smiled up at him. "I'd like that. Thanks. Also, thanks for the tour of the neighborhood. Everything and everyone here is so stable and settled. This was a great idea."

"Yes, I love it here. This community is a place I can really call home. All I need to make my life complete now is a dog." And a wife. He'd made that prayer so often, he now wondered if maybe the time he was spending with Celeste was an answer in progress.

After a short visit into the store, Adrian continued the neighborhood tour.

During the time they walked past a row of new homes under construction where he had no input or history, he decided to change the subject. "You're going to be able to play at the evening service, tonight, too, aren't you?"

"Yes. I realized when I agreed to be part of the team that there were two services on Sundays."

"Great. You already know that it's a bit different, more informal, at the evening service."

"Yes."

"You're so natural in a group and in front of people. It took a long time for me to stop my knees from knocking when everyone was watching me, even though they're not going to church to watch us. I know we're not there for entertainment, but the congregation is still looking forward. When everyone's attention isn't on the words, they do watch us. Sometimes I still find it unnerving. You were great up there this morning. How do you do it?"

Celeste's back stiffened as she walked. She sipped her drink, and took a long time before she finally spoke. When she did, her voice held a note of restraint. "I've done this kind of thing before, actually. So it's not a new experience for me."

"Really? I thought you've never been on a worship team before."

Her voice lowered even more. "It wasn't a worship team. It was a band, and it, uh, didn't have anything to do with church."

"Still, that must have been fun."

"It started out as fun, but there were a few problems. We...broke up."

Her hesitation gave him the impression that there was more to the story. He walked alongside her in silence, waiting for her to elaborate. When she didn't, Adrian chose not to question her further, in case she considered it invasive or prying. He supposed she would tell him later, if it was something he was meant to know.

Since he wasn't sure how much walking she did in the course of a week, Adrian began the journey back to Celeste's home. At their present speed, the entire walk would take approximately two hours, which would leave just the right amount of time to have supper together before it was time to go back to church for the evening service.

Adrian didn't think of himself as a talkative person, but with Celeste, the conversation never lagged. As they walked, they talked about everything and anything, both fun and serious. They even had a rousing discussion about an issue in a book they'd both recently read and enjoyed.

When they arrived back at Celeste's front door, he didn't want them to go their separate ways.

After she'd unlocked and opened the door, he followed her inside, without an invitation, something he'd never done to anyone except the guys. "Even though the tour is done, I hate to end the day. How would you like to join me for dinner? Then we can go straight back to church for the service."

His heart pounded while he waited for her answer.

She smiled hesitantly, then looked up at him, her beautiful green eyes big and wide and strangely serious, considering the last thing she'd said was a joke she'd been told at work. "That sounds like fun. Just let me get my purse, and I'll lock up."

Celeste wrapped up the last cord, pressed the fastener closed to secure it, and tossed the bundle of cords into the carry-all. The stage area was ready for the next group who would be meeting at the church. With school back in session, all the groups were beginning to meet again after the summer break. The children's drama group would be the first to use the stage on Monday, and they were looking forward to another year of fun.

Fun.

In the last month, Celeste found she'd redefined the word. She thought she'd had fun before, after she'd had enough to drink or numbed her brain with enough drugs. The world had rushed by in a stream of activity, color and noise. Sometimes she remembered the night before, sometimes she didn't. When she didn't, she knew she must have had fun, otherwise her brain wouldn't have been in a fog until mid afternoon. Or so she'd thought. Now she wondered if she'd really had as much fun as she thought.

Lately, she'd enjoyed herself in ways she'd never thought possible, like working on her car. She hadn't known that besides being a mechanic, Bob was part owner of a shop. Adrian, Randy and Paul didn't know much about cars, but they helped Bob give her mother's car a tune up, and they took apart and adjusted a number of things Bob said would help. While it was by no means perfect, it ran better than it had before. Bob put a few requests for parts in to some of the auto wreckers he knew. When they came, the five of them would again take the engine apart and put it back together.

While she'd seen men work on cars before, she'd never seen it done without at least a few cases of beer. This time, when they were done, all the men could still walk in a straight line, and there were no leftover parts on the ground. She'd heard no bad language, and instead of frustrated grunts and eventually fistfights, the four men laughed and teased each other all day long. Even though she didn't know anything about cars, they'd included her. Bob even showed her what they were doing, not that she'd understood anything he said.

The next time they'd practiced together, she'd made a wistful comment that she wished she could afford to buy a computer. Then she found out that Randy worked at an electronics store. He said the store regularly bought lots of older computers to be reconditioned from businesses who were upgrading, and he would keep his eye open for a good deal for her.

She immediately reiterated that she couldn't afford it, but each one of them told her how Adrian had helped them plan budgets that were easy to stick to, and suggested that she should do the same.

So, though it was slightly humiliating, but probably good for her, Adrian picked through her finances. Since she had finally passed the probationary period with her employer, she hoped she could now get a small amount of credit, because she was in the position of having a steady full-time job, officially, for the first time in her life.

At first she'd been hesitant to show Adrian something so personal, but what he was looking at was just numbers, on paper, not the intimate details of her personal life. The final factor that convinced her was when Adrian told her that he also did his friends' income tax, including the corporate records and income tax for Bob's business.

Being very businesslike, Adrian calculated her income against all her expenses and spending habits, told her how she could save a little money, how much she could afford, and suggested a couple of types of loan plans that would give her the best bang for her buck, should she be accepted for credit.

On the down side, Adrian now knew not only how little money she made at her job, but she also had to tell him that she only worked in the mail room, a lowly position with a pay scale to match. Younger people she worked with held positions far above her in the structure of the company, but they had more years of working experience. This was the first office job she'd ever done, and the first real job she'd had since a few years past high school, when the only jobs she'd done were at the local fast-food outlets. Fortunately, Adrian didn't ask how she'd supported herself over the last nine years. She continued to tell herself that she'd lost a lot of years, and she had a lot of catching up to do. This was one of the many prices to pay.

But, everything she was doing was worth it.

Tomorrow, after work, she was going shopping.

Randy Reynolds straightened the stack of remote control trucks and stood back to admire his handiwork.

The hour around supper time was traditionally the slowest time at the store. Fortunately, since it was his week to come in early and open up, he only had half an hour left, and he could soon go home.

"Nice job. Very artistic," a familiar voice sounded from behind him.

Randy spun around. "Hey, Adrian, Celeste. Good to see you."

They both smiled in unison at him.

Randy smiled and straightened his tie. He'd found the perfect computer for Celeste. It was an older, reconditioned model with not enough memory to play all the games kids wanted to play, but for the average adult who didn't play games, it had more than enough RAM, a good sound card, a fairly new CD ROM drive and an internal modem.

Since Adrian and Celeste probably weren't there to invite him to join them for dinner, that meant Adrian had found a way to fit the computer into Celeste's budget, if the price was right, and Randy knew it was.

Celeste glanced at the brand-new display for the latest state-of-the-art computer, sighed, then turned back to Randy. "I signed up for night school today, so I'm going to need that computer you told Adrian about."

Randy smiled back. "It's all fixed up and ready. Let me check the book and I'll see how much I can let it go for."

While Randy paged through the book, out of the corner of his eye, he watched Adrian and Celeste together.

Of course he liked Celeste—they all did. All of the guys spent random amounts of time with her, and they always enjoyed themselves when they did.

However, it had recently come to light that the time she spent with Adrian wasn't as random as was the time with the rest of them. For starters, every Friday, without fail, Celeste and Adrian went to the library together. Also, lately, whenever one of them wanted to talk to Adrian and he wasn't home, they somehow always found him at Celeste's house. When they couldn't find Celeste, they usually found her at Adrian's house.

For years, the four of them had all joked that Adrian would probably be the first of all of them to settle down. It looked as if their predictions were coming true. However, the situation gave Randy cause for concern. No one, Adrian included, knew much about Celeste. While she was the answer to their prayers for a talented musician to help them with the worship team, it was as if she had appeared out of nowhere.

As much as Randy liked her, he didn't think God had suddenly created Celeste out of dust just for them. He wanted to know where she'd come from, even if Adrian didn't. In fact, it was making him nervous that Adrian seemed unconcerned about the past details of her life. It wasn't like Adrian to be content to know nothing. He was always the first to clamor for information about any given topic.

When Randy's life had been at its worst, it was Adrian who had been there the most for him, more than Paul or even Bob, because it was in Adrian's personality to be helpful, regardless whether Adrian understood the problem. When Adrian didn't understand the problem, it was in his nature to dig deeper. Randy would never forget what Adrian had done for him. Adrian had been more help to him than he would ever realize. And now, because Adrian wasn't behaving in his normal patterns, Randy wanted to dig deeper to help Adrian, especially if Adrian didn't know he needed it.

Adrian's voice broke Randy out of his mental musings. "Well? How long does it take to look up a price? Do you have bad news?"

Randy shook his head. "Sorry. I was thinking about something and got distracted." He mentioned the lowest price the manager said they could let the unit in question go for. When he saw Celeste's raised eyebrows, he told the story of how he convinced his manager to let her pay in three installments, with no interest, something they usually only did for preferred customers.

Celeste narrowed her eyes. Randy could see her figuring out if the numbers could fit into her budget.

"I think I can do that." She turned her head and looked up at Adrian. "Adrian showed me how I could squeeze that into my budget, and I've been really trying hard to save money. It's close, but it's under the magic number since I can do it in payments. So…" Her voice trailed off, she smiled, and pulled her checkbook out of her purse.

Adrian smiled as if Celeste buying an old reconditioned computer was a major triumph. "Of course you can do it. I knew Randy would give you a good deal."

She turned back to Randy. Her smile was so heartfelt and so beautiful, the required suggestion of the extended warranty for an extra cost didn't come out. She reached forward and rested her fingers on his arm, and gave it a gentle squeeze.

He shuffled back, lowered his head, and made a note in the book that he'd sold the unit. "Don't worry about the extended warranty," he mumbled. "If anything goes wrong, I'll fix it for you."

"Thanks, Randy. You're a pal."

Randy looked up at Adrian. Randy might have been a 'pal,' but he wondered what Celeste considered Adrian to be.

"Can we take it home now?"

"Sure, except I'm alone in the store for another twenty minutes, so I can't help you carry it to the car."

Celeste paused and again looked up at Adrian.

Adrian turned and smiled down at Celeste, who was smiling back up at him. "That's okay. I think we can manage."

Randy narrowed his eyes. It wasn't Adrian who was giving her the good deal on the computer, it was him.

If he'd suspected earlier that there was something big going on between Adrian and Celeste, this confirmed it.

Naturally Randy didn't mind, if that was what his friend really wanted. But, Adrian was acting so out of character, Randy wasn't sure if Adrian knew what he was doing. Adrian always went with the sure thing, never took chances. He always told them more than they wanted to know about any woman he might have considered dating.

Adrian hadn't said a word about Celeste. And for the time he'd spent with Celeste without Adrian, she hadn't questioned them about him, either.

Randy punched the information for the bill into the computer, and waited for Celeste to make out the check for the first payment. As he typed, his boss's words echoed through his head, stressing that his friend had better pay on time, or he was holding Randy personally responsible for the cost of the unit.

He told himself he was doing the right thing as he hit the print button, and handed the invoice to Celeste.

"I guess you can wait out here, and I'll take Adrian into the back to get the computer."

Both of them nodded. Like Chip and Dale.

"Come on, Adrian. This way."

Adrian waited one step inside the doorway, while Randy searched for the unit on the stockroom shelves. "You want a box, or do you just want to take it as it is?"

"We're going straight to Celeste's place, so we don't need a box."

Randy reached behind the monitor and gathered up the cord, not facing Adrian as he spoke. "You're sure doing a lot with Celeste lately. Is there something going on between you two that I don't know about?"

"I don't know how to answer that. Why are you asking?"

"Didn't your mother ever tell you never to answer a question with a question?"

"Maybe. But it's a brilliant way to avoid answering."

Randy turned around. After a response like that, Randy expected Adrian to be smiling, but Adrian was more serious than Randy had seen in a long time.

"What's up with you two? While we all like her, I'm not saying I want to date her. She's not my type. At least I don't think she's my type. What I'm trying to say is I don't know what type she is."

"If you're trying to warn me that she might be a scam artist, I can tell you that she's not. She hasn't singled me out to try to take me for my money. Except for meals, she outright refuses to accept anything from me, especially financial help. I offered to loan her the money for the computer, since it's really cheap, at least from my perspective. She refused."

Randy instantly felt better. "I know what you mean. She wouldn't let me buy her a ticket for that concert Bob and I went to a few weeks ago."

Hearts in Harmony

Adrian nodded back. "I tried to give her a few books I thought she'd like. She was very insistent that she was only borrowing them, not keeping them. I've seen her bank balance, too. She really is as broke as she looks."

Randy glanced to the door, just to make sure that Celeste hadn't wondered what was taking so long, and decided to check on them. "Yeah, but that electric grand piano she's got isn't cheap. I wonder where she got it?"

Adrian stiffened. "I hope you're not inferring that it's stolen. She would never do such a thing."

"Are you sure? What exactly do you know about her?"

Adrian glanced toward the doorway, then back to Randy. He paused for a few seconds before finally speaking. "I don't know much of her history before we met, but I do know that she's honest and honorable, and she continues to grow in her walk with the Lord. We enjoy the same things, and we like the same books and movies. She laughs at my jokes and I laugh at hers. Even when we don't see eye to eye on things, which we don't all the time, we can agree to disagree, and move on. She sounds like she works hard at her job, and she's doing well at school, despite what she says about how hard she has to study. It's a difficult course she's taking. She really has more potential than she gives herself credit for. I just feel we've made a connection. Yet at the same time, she seems so lost…and alone."

Randy stared at his friend. This was much more than he needed to know. It also told him that Adrian was in way over his head, and there was nothing Randy could do about it, except be there to pick up the pieces.

Randy cleared his throat. "I hope you know what you're doing."

Adrian didn't reply, which unfortunately gave Randy his answer. Knowing he wouldn't get any more information out of Adrian, Randy turned around and picked up the tower and the keyboard. "This doesn't come with a printer. She'll probably need one."

"I told her to put her data on a disk and use mine when she needs to print something. She really can't afford it. I just wish she'd open up to me. I've got a gut feeling there's something she needs to talk about, and she won't."

Together, they turned toward the door. Randy wanted to wish Adrian good luck. He had a feeling Adrian was going to need it.

Chapter Seven

"What's this?"

Celeste nearly dropped the spoon into the pot. She spun around to see Adrian standing in the doorway, holding up her attempt at a hobby.

"It's called cross stitch. Can't you tell? Or is it that bad?"

He laughed softly. Something in her stomach fluttered, telling her that she was more hungry than she thought.

"It's not bad, and of course I can tell. But I didn't want to go snooping through that plastic bag you've got on the floor, so I don't know what it's eventually going to look like. These flowers are nice, but they look like a border, rather than the main theme."

Celeste groaned out loud. "For a border, it's harder than it looks. A few weeks ago Paul took me to a craft store so he could buy some extra stuff for the kids in his class. While I was waiting, I was looking at something the owner had hanging on the wall. She called it a sampler. That's when you've got words, surrounded by flowers and designs and stuff. When I told her how much I liked hers, she showed me how to do it. She said it's really relaxing. She was very nice, and said she would make the pattern for me on her computer if I bought all the thread and stuff at the store. So I did. I picked my favorite Bible verse, and this way I can have something to hang on the wall that's really mine. Also, it gives me something to do in my spare time."

"As if you have extra time between…" Adrian raised his hands and started counting on his fingers, "…Bible study on Mondays, night-school classes Tuesdays and Thursdays, let's not forget time to study, and worship team practice on Wednesdays. I hope you don't intend to stay home and do this on Fridays instead of going to the library with me. And when exactly do you have time to read those books we get at the library?"

"Actually, I take a book to work and read on my breaks."

He smiled. "I see you're taking my suggestion seriously, that taking a lunch from home instead of going out saves major money in the course of a month."

She nodded. Adrian didn't know that she always stayed in the building during her lunch breaks, but it wasn't strictly to save money. The money was a side bonus, not that she didn't need it. The real reason was because the high-rise office tower was enclosed and safe from prying eyes.

"Yes. But even if I don't have any spare time, I do my cross stitch for about half an hour every night, before bed. When I read, it gets me thinking of so many things at once, it's hard to focus in on one subject. Every day I need the reminder that in God's eyes I'm a new creation, especially after I've had a bad day and feel like giving up. It's not a simple 'God loves me' type of verse. Pastor Ron explained this to me. When I accepted Jesus as my Savior, my soul was restored, and I was made new."

Celeste smiled from ear to ear. She was glad the old Celeste was gone. Admittedly some days were better than others, especially when her thoughts drifted back to Zac and the way she used to be with him. She knew she wasn't good enough to be in God's presence. But God Himself promised that her past sins were washed away when she gave her heart to Jesus. From that day forward, she could start over and not look back.

Except she did look back. Often. She was hoping having the sampler in plain sight would help her get her head back on straight again. She could believe it, because God had promised. And unlike men, God didn't break His promises.

She cleared her throat and turned around to continue stirring their supper. "But you know that cross stitch isn't as relaxing as the woman claimed, especially when I make a mistake and have to take a section apart. But the more I do, the more I want to finish. In a way, it's almost addicting." She didn't know much about crafts and cross stitch, but she was learning the hard way, just as she'd also learned about other, more serious addictions the hard way. Only this addiction, she could handle.

"My mother does this kind of thing. You should see some of the stuff she's done. In fact, you should come over to my parents' place one day. Although, I have a sneaking suspicion that once you tell her you've started a cross-stitch project, she'll never let you go. My mother would love to meet you, crafts aside, of course."

This time, Celeste did drop the spoon into the stew. She

pressed one hand over her heart and spun around. "You want me to meet your parents?"

He shrugged his shoulders, and his expression suddenly turned hesitant. "Mom's been teasing me because every time she calls lately, she gets my voicemail. She's curious to see who I've been spending so much time with. I have to admit I told her a little about you. Remember, when you first joined the worship team, the whole church was talking about you, and word naturally traveled back to the home church."

Her stomach lurched. Suddenly, instead of feeling hungry, she felt sick. "The other church is talking about me? The big one?"

Adrian moved toward her, laid her cross-stitch project on the table, and continued until he was only one step away. "Don't worry, it's only good things. They're saying how you've added so much to the service, and how badly we needed you. I heard that the music director wants us to do a guest visit at the home church, because the congregation wants to see us in action."

Celeste's head swam. While she knew she was putting herself on display, she had thought the church was a closed circle. She hadn't considered that the bigger parent church would also have an interest. In hindsight, it only made sense.

She took a few deep breaths to calm down. Even though she was a new creation, now and for the future, she couldn't yet forget about her past. She had to be realistic when putting herself on display. She told herself every time she went up to the front that Zac didn't know anyone who attended church or in any way considered the name of God to be anything other than one of many creative and colorful curses.

Again Celeste begged God's forgiveness. Not long ago, she'd been no different than Zac. Yes, she was new, but she wasn't that new.

"Celeste? Is something wrong?"

"No, it's okay. But I was wondering, how long has this talk been going on?"

"People started talking about you after the first service, but don't worry. No one would ever say anything except nice things. "

Her blood ran cold. Not that Adrian knew of, anyway.

He stepped closer. Very gently, Adrian rested both his palms on her shoulders. One corner of his mouth tilted up, in a warm, half smile. "You seem so comfortable up at the front, I would never have guessed you'd be so nervous with a bigger congregation. They're all very nice people, but it's okay. I'll just tell him we're not ready, and we'll do it some time in the future."

Celeste was shocked by the sudden and unexpected sensation from the warmth of Adrian's hands on her shoulders. In all the time they'd known each other, they'd never touched. She'd made sure of it. But now, the gentle way he held her showed his inner strength. If she wanted to move away, he would release her in a second. She knew it.

She tilted her head up to look into his eyes, where all she saw was tenderness and concern.

She couldn't help it. Her lower lip started to quiver.

At the slight quirk of his eyebrows, she could tell that he noticed. "It's okay," he mumbled. "Come here."

Slowly, his arms slipped down her back, but he didn't draw her closer. Instead, he hesitated, and she knew he was waiting for an indication of what she wanted, and how far she would allow him to go. By his actions, or lack thereof, Celeste knew without a doubt that Adrian would never force her to do anything she didn't want to do, and he would never press her beyond where she felt comfortable.

To answer his unspoken question, Celeste slipped her hands around him and leaned into his chest. Adrian tightened his embrace slightly, then pressed his cheek to her temple. Slowly and gently, he rubbed tender circles on her back. Knowing that he would do no more than hold her filled Celeste with an unbelievable case of the warm fuzzies, comforting her in a way she'd never felt in her life.

It felt so good, she didn't know what to think. She'd never felt this way with Zac, not even when things were good, or at least when she thought they were good.

But one thing she did know; being like this now forced her to admit to herself that she'd never known real trust. If she'd had any doubts before, she now knew for sure that she had fallen in love with Adrian Braithwaite: accountant, mediocre musician and all-around nice guy. For a minute, she let herself fantasize that she could have a normal life with him—marriage, a house, kids, even a dog, as he wanted. However, she knew it couldn't happen. He wasn't perfect, but he was still too good for a woman like her. But for a few minutes, she could pretend it was possible.

Adrian's voice broke her out of dreamland. "I think it's time to stir the stew, and we should eat or we're going to be late."

He released her and stepped back. A rush of cool air replaced the warmth where they'd been pressed together, immediately making her regret that they were both obligated to be elsewhere very soon.

Before he could read anything from her expression, Celeste turned and used a ladle to scoop out the spoon she'd dropped into the pot. "Bring me the plates, and I'll just fill them up from here."

"Good idea. That way we'll also have fewer dishes to do."

He was so good to her; he even helped with the dishes. He never yelled at her. Instead of becoming impatient and calling her stupid when she didn't understand something, he explained what she needed to know, slowly and gently.

She didn't know why God had put Adrian in her life, but she thanked Him daily.

As he did every time they ate together, Adrian said a short prayer of thanks for their food. They ate quickly and dashed off to the Sunday-evening service, with Adrian insisting that he would come back when everything was over and help her clean up.

Unlike every other time he made the offer, this time, she didn't argue.

"Bye, Adrian. See you tomorrow night!"

Adrian waved back at Paul as Paul slid the microphones into the padded case.

Tonight had been a good night, not much different than any other Sunday-evening service. The worship time had gone well. Pastor Ron had delivered a good message, and Randy got his favorite kind of donut before one of the youths beat him to it.

But tonight, *Celeste* had been different. The evening service was always more relaxed than the more formal morning service, but Celeste was tenser.

Something was wrong. He didn't know what it was, he only knew that something was bothering her.

Adrian watched Celeste throw a cord into the case and snap the fastener closed.

He stepped beside her before she could think of a way to change her mind about their earlier agreement. "Let's go back to your place now. The rest of the guys are going to pack everything into the closets."

"But—"

Adrian raised his palms in the air to stop her protests. "They don't mind, I've already asked. This way we don't have to rush. I know we only have a few dishes, but I think we both need a little time to relax tonight."

She smiled weakly. "Okay. I guess."

He almost said that he would be content to just sit and watch her do her cross stitch, but he didn't think she was in the mood for jokes. Besides, the way he was feeling, he really would have sat and watched her do something so mundane, just to be with her.

As on every other Sunday evening, Celeste picked up Adrian's guitar case, Adrian picked up the case with Celeste's electric piano, and they began their trip to the parking lot and Adrian's car.

The trip back to her home was made in silence. They barely talked at all during the short cleanup. It wasn't unusual, but this time, it bothered Adrian.

He tucked the dish towel over the oven handle, and watched Celeste as she drained the sink.

Finally, he couldn't stand it anymore. He moved toward her until he was so close he could have touched her, but he didn't. "Celeste, what's wrong?"

She spun around quickly. When she tilted her head up to look at him, her eyes made her look like a deer that had been caught in the headlights.

He waited for well over a minute before she finally spoke. "Nothing's wrong. I just have a few things to think about."

Something about her lost expression tied his heart up in knots. He thought about how he'd held her in his arms earlier, and how it had made everything feel better, at least temporarily. She'd been a perfect fit, and he hadn't known a hug could feel so good. He couldn't not touch her now.

He reached forward to gently rest his hands on her shoulders. It wasn't enough.

Just like before, he started to draw her in for a hug, but this time, he knew how good it was going to be. As she came to him, he looked down at her.

That was his mistake. Her eyes drifted halfway closed, and her pouty little mouth showed just the hint of a contented smile.

He couldn't not kiss her.

Instead of pulling her close toward him, he kept one hand on her shoulder, and with the other, he tilted her chin up slightly with one finger. He wanted to kiss her, but he wouldn't without permission. Her eyes opened, and he stared into them, lost in their depths, hoping that he didn't look like a besotted fool, as he tried to think of something appropriate to say.

Celeste's voice dropped to a ragged whisper. "Oh, Adrian, I—" Her words broke off as she raised herself on her toes. Her palms cupped his cheeks, she leaned in closer and kissed him. Deeply and fully.

Adrian froze, but not for long. As soon as he got over the shock, he lowered his hands to embrace her fully and matched the enthusiasm of her mouth on his, kissing her back with all his heart and soul. The gentle touch of her soft hands on his face made his heart pound as she kissed him passionately, holding him captive in a way he'd never experienced before.

The pressure of her mouth on his gradually lessened, until they had almost separated, but not quite. With their lips still touching just enough to feel the brush of their softness, Adrian started to tilt his head to kiss her again. Before he could make full contact her tongue flicked his lower lip, she gave it a little nibble, her hands drifted down to his chest, and she kissed him again.

A flush of exhilaration coursed through him. Not that he'd never kissed a woman before, but he'd never been in a relationship where the woman was so enthusiastic, so enticing, or so aggressive. Every other time he'd kissed a woman he was dating, the experience had been chaste and…boring.

Celeste's kisses were anything but boring. Fireworks went off in his brain when her hands moved again, this time to rest on his hips, without Celeste easing up on her kisses.

Every coherent thought in his head evaporated. He thought he should shift positions, but his brain wasn't connecting with the rest of him to allow him to do anything.

Just as he finally managed to move one hand on her back, Celeste began to release his mouth, so slowly it was almost painful. Short of behaving like a caveman and grabbing her to pull her back, he couldn't think enough to figure out what he could do to keep her there.

The situation was spinning out of control. At first, he'd thought she was going to say she loved him, but she'd kissed him instead of talking. And it was much more than just a simple kiss. He was wired from the top of his head all the way down to his toes. He hoped she'd said with actions what he wanted to hear with words, because he felt the same way.

Adrian's heart pounded at the realization. He was in love. Between the discovery of how much he loved her and the mind-numbing fervor of her kisses, he felt as if he'd been poleaxed.

Slowly, Celeste's eyes opened, eyes a man could drown in. Beautiful eyes, the color of polished jade, unique, just like the person whose heart they reflected.

She blinked a few times, and her eyes cleared. "Adrian? Are you okay?"

Adrian sucked in a deep breath to regulate his ragged breathing. He wanted to kiss her again, only this time he was ready and primed for more, because he knew what to expect. Yet, he knew they'd stepped into dangerous territory. His heart was pounding, and all his senses were on edge. He needed to hold her, to kiss her and to be kissed by her so bad it hurt. But if they continued, he didn't know that they would be able to stop, and that would be wrong. He'd never needed to exercise control more than this at any point in his life.

"Yeah, uh, I…" He tugged at his collar. "It must be hot in here," he said, only half joking.

Of course, one look at him would tell her that he wasn't okay, and she was looking. He grinned weakly. "Wow," was the best he could come up with.

Her face paled, and she backed up. "You know, it's getting a little late, and I'm awfully tired. I think it would be best if you went home."

"Home?" Adrian checked his watch. It wasn't late. Most Sunday evenings at this time, they would have still been at the church, packing up. Usually the five of them went out for coffee and donuts afterward, especially if Randy didn't get his favorite kind of donut before the youth group stormed through the refreshment area. "But…"

His protests froze in his throat. Her eyes widened and her whole body tensed, as if she was about to run—she looked just like the scared out-of-gas rabbit he'd found at the side of the highway not that long ago.

He didn't understand what had happened, but tonight a line had been crossed. He thought they should probably talk about it, but Celeste suddenly looked as if she didn't even want to be in the same room with him.

Adrian didn't know what he'd done wrong. It wasn't as though he'd done anything she didn't want to do. Celeste had started it—she'd kissed him as he'd never been kissed before. However, with the way everything so quickly spiraled out of control, they both obviously had a lot of thinking to do. He didn't have enough experience with women in general to know what he was supposed to do next.

Adrian stiffened, cleared his throat and rammed his hands into his pockets. "I guess you're right. Goodnight, Celeste."

Even though he knew he shouldn't, Adrian wanted to kiss her again at the door, on his way out, now that he knew the potential. Instead, the door closed gently behind him before he had a chance to turn around.

She didn't want to see him any more tonight, but at least he would see her the following evening, when he would pick her up for the Monday-night Bible study meeting.

Chapter Eight

Adrian jumped high in the air, catching the ball meant for Randy. He landed squarely, bounced the basketball once, and even though he knew he was beyond his optimum throwing range from the hoop, he tossed it anyway.

All the movement in the gymnasium stopped as Paul, Randy and Bob watched the ball arc, then begin its descent.

Adrian held his breath as the ball hit the ring, circled once, twice, and then fell to the side.

"Wow. Nice try," Bob muttered from beside him. Tonight, Bob and Adrian were teammates for the evening for a game of two-on-two against Randy and Paul. Because Adrian hadn't scored, Bob took off at a fast run to recover the ball before Randy or Paul could reach it.

Randy, however, didn't run. "I've never seen you try a shot from so far away, but that was really close. Have you been practicing without us? You haven't made it out the last few times. I expected you to be worse, not better."

"I've had other stuff to do on Tuesday nights," Adrian mumbled, then took off to guard Bob against Paul. The four of them tried to meet once a month in the basement of the church, which was a small gymnasium, to play basketball. It was something they all looked forward to, although lately Bob hadn't been as regular as in the past because he needed to spend more time working at his business. The last couple of months Adrian hadn't been as regular, either, but Adrian's absence had nothing to do with work.

Randy also took off at a run, but not after the ball, which was now in Bob's possession. Randy followed Adrian.

At the hoop, Bob bounced the ball once, took aim, and jumped. Being more stocky and not as tall as Adrian, Bob couldn't jump as high, but he was much closer to the hoop than Adrian had been. Bob did manage to score, which meant that as soon as the ball dropped from the hoop, it was free for Paul or Randy.

Randy made no move forward, either for the ball or toward Bob to keep him away from Paul, who was now dribbling the ball down the length of the small gym toward the other basket. Adrian took off after Paul. Again, Randy followed Adrian.

"Shouldn't you be over there?" Adrian called out over his shoulder as he jogged.

"No way," Randy panted behind him. "I want to know what you're doing here."

Adrian ran a little faster, but Randy still continued to shadow him. "I'm playing basketball, in case you can't tell," he mumbled, this time not turning his head as he picked up his speed.

Randy's panting became more pronounced, but he didn't stop running. "I meant, why aren't you doing whatever else it is you've been doing on Tuesday nights lately? Is Celeste busy or something?"

Suddenly the room went silent except for Adrian and Randy's footsteps. The distinct rap of the ball sharply hitting the hardwood floor once echoed through the room. Paul's voice reverberated through the near-empty expanse. "Randy! Here!"

The ball hurtled in Randy's direction. However, as Randy raised his arms to catch it, Adrian barged in front of Randy, caught the ball, then took off, dribbling it back in the other direction.

"Randy!" Paul shouted. "That's twice in a row! What are you doing?"

Adrian didn't look behind him. He quickly approached the basket, jumped and shot the ball, this time scoring a basket.

From the other side of the court, Bob let out a big whoop.

Since Randy was closer than Paul, Adrian caught the ball after it dropped from the basket and sent it in Randy's direction. Randy bounced it once and started to dribble it back down to the other side, but Adrian knew that Randy was already winded.

With a burst of speed, Adrian ignored his pounding heart and the fact that he was also starting to pant fairly heavily as well. He caught up to Randy, smacked the ball away, bounced it once and threw it to Bob.

"Hey!" Randy exclaimed, finally starting to sound annoyed. "What's with you? Knock it off!"

A trickle of moisture dribbled down Adrian's chest beneath his T-shirt, which was already soaked. He couldn't remember ever being so sweaty, but instead of being disgusted, he felt invigorated. Motivated. Strong. He felt no guilt from taking advantage of Randy. Adrian wasn't usually so aggressive, but today Randy annoyed him. It had started with Randy's wisecrack that he was there only because Celeste was busy.

It didn't help that Randy was right.

Bob caught the ball easily, and began to dribble it to the hoop. Paul skidded to a halt and stared at Bob, who, in his mind, shouldn't have had the ball at that moment.

Adrian smirked. Paul played basketball often with the pre-teens at the school where he taught. Naturally, all the kids were shorter and slower than he was. Because Paul loved kids, he allowed himself to be sloppy with his techniques in order to let the kids win. During their monthly basketball skirmishes, it always took Paul a while to shape up and get used to adult competition. Bob was taking full advantage of the situation until that happened.

Paul took off in a run for Bob, but Adrian knew it was futile. Not only was Bob in great shape, he had the most stamina of all four of them. Between the heavy lifting he did at his auto shop, plus the longer and longer hours as his business increased, Bob quickly became single-mindedly focused when faced with a demanding task, whether business or pleasure.

Again, at just the right spot in front of the hoop, a second before Paul reached him, Bob jumped and sank another basket.

Adrian didn't know why Bob was playing extra hard today, but between the two of them, they were a team that couldn't be beat.

When the clock hit the top of the hour, the time they'd agreed to quit, Paul sank back against the wall. Like Randy, Paul had been completely overwhelmed with the degree of competition between the two sides. Today, Adrian had played to win, and he had. By a lot.

Adrian lifted his glasses and swiped his arm across his forehead as he walked toward Paul, catching a drip just before it went into his eye. "Good game!" he called out.

"Better for some," Paul grunted as he pushed himself away from the wall and started walking toward the door.

Adrian caught up with Paul and they continued on their way together.

Physical exhaustion was starting to replace the exhilaration of a good game and a good win. The rush he'd enjoyed on the basketball court was now fading back to reality, but Adrian didn't want that to happen so soon.

Once in the hall, Paul headed straight for the water fountain. He drank deeply, then cupped one hand, filled it with water, dumped the water on top of his head, and rubbed it into his hair. He stood straight, and turned around to face Adrian. "Wanna talk about it?" he asked, ignoring the water streaming down his cheeks.

As best friends, he and Paul talked about everything and anything. He'd been the first of his friends to actually own his own home, versus renting and he had spent hours with Paul discussing the wisdom of buying a house as a single person before he made his final decision to actually purchase. Now, however, he didn't want to share his thoughts. The intimate details of his house and his budget were one thing, but opening his heart was quite another.

"I don't know what you mean," was the best he could come up with.

Paul glanced over Adrian's shoulder to the door leading to the gym, then focused back on Adrian's face.

"What's bothering you? I thought you were going to do harm to poor Randy."

As if saying his name made him appear, the door opened, and Randy's voice sounded. "Hey, Adrian, how's your love life?"

Adrian clenched his fists and spun around, expecting to see Randy wearing a cocky grin, which would be the last straw for Adrian to show his friend exactly what he thought of him sticking his nose where it didn't belong. Instead, Randy's expression was very serious. Bob stood beside Randy, saying nothing.

Randy stood in silence, waiting patiently, a first for him.

Adrian blinked. All his anger diffused, if not his frustration. "My love life isn't open for discussion," he grumbled.

Randy shrugged his shoulders. "Ah. But the fact that you say your love life isn't open at least proves that you finally have one. Speaking of Celeste, how is she? I noticed she wasn't at the Bible study meeting last night."

Adrian vividly recalled the last time he'd seen Celeste, which was Sunday night, only two evenings ago.

At the thought of the way they'd kissed, his heart started beating almost as hard as it had on the basketball court, and he all but groaned out loud at the poignant memory.

He hadn't entirely been driven by his hormones. His brain and his heart were equally involved, which made the experience even more potent. He had a gut feeling that she had been caught off guard by the power of the moment, too. For him, the heat that had flared between them meant only one thing, and that was that she loved him just as much as he loved her.

Except she'd kicked him out, and he hadn't seen her

since. On Monday, she'd missed the Bible study meeting, and then today, Tuesday, she told him not to bother waiting for her when she got off night school, because she wouldn't need any help with her homework. Also, as if that wasn't bad enough, she'd said she was too tired to stay up for tea and donuts, which was what they did most Tuesdays and Thursdays when he picked her up from night school.

It didn't make sense. He'd even prayed about it, but he hadn't received an answer.

The silence dragged. Paul was the first to speak. "This looks serious. Did you two have a fight?"

"No," Adrian answered quickly. The last time he'd seen her, what they'd done was the farthest thing from a fight he could possibly think of.

As soon as the word left his mouth, three sets of raised eyebrows told him that he'd spoken too fast.

He glared at his friends. Silence hung in the air.

Bob finally spoke. "Methinks there's trouble in paradise."

Adrian thought back to how his relationship with Celeste had developed since the first time they met. They were together every day of the week. In the time since they'd met, he'd come to know her better than any woman he'd ever dated. In many ways, he wondered if he knew her better than some of his lifelong friends. As much as he liked her as a friend, he was also very attracted to her as a woman. In all the ways he knew her, he loved her.

But at the same time, she always changed the subject when he tried to talk about anything that had happened before the day he had picked her up on the deserted Country Meadows Highway.

And that wasn't the way it was supposed to be in paradise.

"It's not like that," he muttered.

"Let me guess," said Bob. "She's acting different all of a sudden, and you can't figure it out."

Adrian straightened his glasses and crossed his arms over his chest, momentarily cringing at touching his sweaty T-shirt, which had become cold and clammy. "How did you know that?"

Bob gave a single, half-hearted laugh. "I have three sisters, remember? And I have an older brother who had a few girlfriends before he finally got married. I've had to listen to a lot of nonsense. I tell you, I'll never put up with that. I've seen too much of it." Bob paused, and also crossed his arms over his chest. "I just find it very strange that Celeste would be that way. She always struck me as someone who doesn't play mind games or have control issues. She's always been very careful not to hurt feelings or step on anyone's toes. It also seems like once she gets herself into a routine, she likes it that way. Kind of like someone else I know."

"You're not helping."

Bob shrugged his shoulders. "But I speak the truth. Did something happen?"

Something had happened, all right, but Adrian wasn't going to share those details with his friends. Based on past experience, when two adults finally crossed the line and kissed for the first time, that opened a relationship up, instead of shutting it down.

"I already said it's not open for discussion."

Randy's mouth opened, but fortunately for him, he closed it again before anything came out.

Paul raised his hand and pushed his wet hair back, and

off his face. "I bumped into Celeste at the drug store to-night on the way home from school. Now that I think about it, she was acting a little funny. She kept glancing over her shoulder, as if she expected someone else would be join-ing us."

Randy broke out into a grin. "You mean like that time before our first practice when she went to grab a burger, and then one at a time, when we saw her car, we all joined her?" Randy's grin widened. "And then we were all late for practice."

Paul didn't smile back. In fact, not only did he not smile, his frown deepened. "I remember that day. But it wasn't like that. She seemed almost nervous. Jumpy." He turned back to Adrian. "You can tell me. What did you do?"

Adrian stiffened. Unconsciously, his voice raised. "I told you, I didn't do anything!"

Paul raised his palms in the air. "Settle down, I'm just asking."

Randy rested his fists on his hips, then turned toward Bob. "I think those two need to talk."

Bob turned to Randy. "Yeah. Tomorrow night is prac-tice. We'll just have to make sure we all leave on time."

Randy nodded. "Maybe we can disconnect one of her spark plugs so after we all leave, she's stuck at Adrian's house."

Bob rolled his eyes. "I'm not doing that. Besides, she only lives a couple of blocks away. She could just walk home."

"Yeah, but then Adrian would have to walk her home."

"Hello?" Adrian stepped forward. "I'm right here."

Randy waved one hand in the air. "Not now. We're talking."

Adrian cleared his throat. "Don't you dare do anything stupid. As bad as that car is, she needs it for work in the morning."

Beside him, Paul snickered. "Don't worry. Randy's all talk. I'm sure you and Celeste will get some time alone tomorrow night. Come on, let's go out for coffee. It's still early, and I could use a sugar fix after a workout like that."

Randy's eyebrows perked, and he spun around. "Did someone say donuts? I'm in."

Adrian peeled off his damp T-shirt and reached into the duffel bag he'd left on the floor for a clean one. He was relieved the subject had been changed. Still, talking about it had confirmed in his own mind that he'd done nothing that was wrong or bad.

Tomorrow was worship team practice night, and Celeste would be there. Once she settled back into the routine, all would return to normal as they resumed their regular patterns.

Although, now knowing what it would be like, he hoped that his friends would do exactly as they suggested and leave early, only without ambushing Celeste's car.

Then, he could once again kiss her.

Adrian smiled all the way to the car.

"Let's pick it up again from the chorus. Celeste, can we have a little more action and something higher on the treble end?"

Celeste nodded at Paul, then moved her right hand up an octave to produce the desired effect.

"Three, four…"

As they began playing together, Celeste couldn't help

but glance at Adrian. Unfortunately, he also glanced at her at the same time.

When their eyes met, Celeste froze. She made a mistake, which created a domino effect. Adrian followed her with a wrong chord, then Paul plucked a string too hard. Randy tried to turn the bass down on the mixing board, but accidentally turned it up instead. He started to laugh, which made Bob miss what was left of the beat. The music ground to a halt.

"Whoa," Paul muttered. "We'd better try that again. Three four…"

This time, as Celeste played she refused to watch anything except her sheet music.

She still couldn't look at Adrian without the memory of the way they'd kissed burning into her mind, heart and soul.

She'd thought she could keep it simple, a quick kiss as an innocent act of affection, but once their lips met she'd been unable to.

Celeste gritted her teeth and held the chord instead of moving it as she'd done in the past, knowing that if she had to do anything that required any concentration, she couldn't.

The situation with Adrian on Sunday night could very easily have spiraled out of control—it almost had, but Adrian had been the one to exercise good judgment. That he had done so shouldn't have been unexpected. He led a moral, upright life, using noble and justifiable restraint in all areas of his life, especially when something could affect his future. That was one of the reasons she loved him so much.

But at the same time, she could tell that compared to her,

he was an inexperienced kisser. She hadn't considered all the ramifications of that knowledge until it was too late.

Out of the corner of her eye, against her better judgment, she glanced quickly at Adrian as he worked on a part she knew he struggled with, knowing that he wouldn't be able to look up at her until he finished that section.

Intense concentration showed on his face and in his stiff posture. Both in the group, and on his own he worked hard and sacrificed his time to do his best for a very worthy cause, which was for the good of the people in his church.

Celeste felt like a deviant. Adrian was innocent in ways she hadn't been since she was fifteen years old. Seducing him the way she had made her worse than the wicked witch with the candy cottage, trying to lure the innocent children to her home in order to eat them for dinner.

Celeste turned back to her music and tried to concentrate on what she should have been doing in the first place. She should have been working on music meant to glorify God—the God who had given her Adrian as the only truly good thing she'd ever had in her life.

Up until Sunday, she'd purposely ignored all the signs. But then, when Adrian moved to kiss her, if it wasn't obvious enough before, it was as blatant as a flashing neon sign telling her exactly where he wanted to go with their relationship.

Up until then she'd done well in keeping things platonic, but in the face of temptation, she'd fallen. Worse she'd almost made Adrian fall right behind her.

She couldn't help but love him. He'd opened up her life in ways she could never have imagined or foreseen, spiritually, socially and emotionally. For the first time, she experienced the simple joy of just being with someone, without necessarily doing anything, even talking. He helped to teach her more about the God who loved her so much and pulled her out of her pit of self-destruction.

But now, in loving Adrian, she'd opened the door to all her past sins, and she'd begun leading Adrian down the path to moral destruction. He deserved someone better than her. He needed someone equal to himself in the eyes of God and man. That woman wasn't her.

Paul's voice broke through the music, bringing everything to a halt again. "Hold on. Adrian, would you like a little time to work on those couple of bars by yourself before we join in?"

"Thanks," Adrian mumbled as he pressed his fingers to the strings, making the chord position, but not playing it. "This won't take long."

Adrian counted down the frets to figure out the right notes, then carefully worked out his fingering to get the right sequence for the few bars he was to play a bit of counter-melody instead of just playing the chords. At the same time, Paul also worked through his own fingering for his part in the difficult section

After watching them for a few seconds Celeste lowered her head, but instead of looking at her keyboard and figuring out her own contribution to the difficult bars, she closed her eyes and prayed.

Dear Lord, Adrian deserves better than me. He deserves a virtuous woman. I can't lead Adrian down the path where I've been. Please, send him the woman who's best for him. Someone with a good and noble heart, just like his.

Paul's voice broke into her thoughts. "Okay, let's do it. Ready?"

This time, they played the section flawlessly. Wanting to end on a positive note, they decided to stop then, which Celeste noted was earlier than usual.

As if he could read her mind, Randy made a rather obvious show of checking his watch. "Wow, look at the time. I have to go. I guess I'll see everyone Sunday morning."

Before Celeste could tell Randy that his watch was wrong, that it wasn't late, it was actually early, Randy was gone.

Without stopping in the kitchen to grab a donut.

She stared at the door, shook her head, then turned back to the room. Paul already had his bass guitar in the case. "I have to go, too. See you all Sunday. Don't be late."

In the blink of an eye, Paul was gone, too.

Bob raised his arms over his head, closed his eyes, and stretched. "I'm really tired. I had a hard day at the shop. I think I'll just leave everything set up here and go home to bed. I'll come early Sunday morning and take everything down then."

Celeste forced herself to breathe. When Bob left, that would leave her alone with Adrian.

The way she was feeling now, all Adrian would have to do was say one nice word, and she would break down and tell him everything. She couldn't allow that to happen. Not now. Not ever. If she told him about how and why she really came to be with them, he'd never want to see her again, and she couldn't deal with that.

She needed time to think, and to pray about what to do.

Celeste cleared her throat, and hoped her voice would come out sounding half normal. "You know, I'm really tired, too. I think I'm also going to go to bed early tonight."

Adrian lowered his guitar into the case. "But—"

Celeste turned off the keyboard. She quickly grabbed her music while Bob tucked his sticks into the tote.

She took a couple of steps toward the door, speaking over her shoulder as she walked. "Tomorrow night I'm going to have coffee with one of the other ladies in the class to discuss a group assignment, so I won't see you after night school."

Adrian stepped forward. "What about Fri—"

Celeste quickened her pace, needing to leave before Bob. "There's something else I have to do," she called out. "But if things change, I'll let you know."

Before Adrian could catch up to her, she hurried out the door and to her car, hoping that Adrian wouldn't follow her, that he would stay in the house to see Bob out.

The car started with a backfire, and she was moving before the cloud of smoke cleared.

When she arrived at home, she could barely get her key into the lock, her hands were shaking so badly.

She was a coward.

Instead of facing her problems, she'd run.

Just like the last time. She'd been scared then, but this time, she was frightened in a different way.

The backs of her eyes started to burn as she pushed the door open.

Last time, she'd had her escape planned. She'd thought about it, determined her options and prepared herself. She'd stated her terms and given Zac her ultimatums, knowing he wouldn't give up his ways to suit God, even though she did get Zac to acknowledge in his own way that God at least did exist. But that wasn't enough for Celeste, so she'd left everything behind. Her work, her hopes, her dreams. Everything she had been striving for. Everything she'd ever known. And she'd started again.

This time, she simply ran, and she had no plan.

She dropped her music on the coffee table, and continued into the kitchen to put on a pot of tea.

Usually, a cup of herbal tea helped relax her. Tonight, she suspected that even a gallon of tea would be of little benefit.

Despite all that she'd given up, nothing hurt so badly as having to end her special relationship with Adrian. She couldn't let it continue in its present course.

As Celeste reached for the kettle, her vision became blurry. She set the kettle down to wipe a layer of moisture away from her eyes.

She almost laughed, except her situation was more pathetic than funny. She was crying. The last time she'd cried was when her father had died, many, many years ago. She hadn't shed a tear about anything since then, basically her whole life.

But then, she'd never met a man like Adrian.

And she never would again.

Chapter Nine

Adrian stared at the pile of books on the coffee table. They wouldn't be returned tonight.

He closed his eyes and gritted his teeth. When had his life deteriorated to the point where the highlight of his week was going to the library on Friday night? Of course it wasn't the library that was so special, it was that he went there with Celeste.

Adrian resisted the urge to whack the books off the coffee table. Instead, he stomped into the kitchen, where he stared blankly at the kettle and the teapot he'd bought just for Celeste.

They wouldn't be used tonight.

Adrian strode back into the living room and flopped down on the couch.

Instead of looking at the television, his gaze fixed on the stuffed teddy bear wearing glasses that he'd perched on top of the entertainment center. Celeste had bought it for him as a joke, saying that it looked like him because not only was the bear wearing glasses, it was also wearing pants

with suspenders. Therefore that meant it was an accountant, like him.

Adrian stared at a spot on the wall. He missed her teasing. He missed everything about her.

All he'd been able to do was think about Celeste. He still
didn't think he'd done anything wrong, but he had narrowed down the time of the change to when she kissed him.
And she had been the one to kiss him, even though he'd
meant to be the first to initiate it. The timing couldn't be a
coincidence, which meant that even though he had thor-
oughly enjoyed the experience, Celeste regretted it.

He couldn't turn back the clock, nor could he pretend it
hadn't happened. He suddenly understood the meaning of the
expression, being caught between a rock and a hard place.

He couldn't do nothing, but he didn't know what to do.

Fortunately, before he had time to fully sink into a quag-
mire of melancholy depression the phone rang. He reached
over and answered it without getting up.

"Hey, Adrian. It's me. Bob. Are you busy?"

The sound of an impact wrench echoed in the background, telling him that Bob and his partner were again
forced to work late on a Friday night. At this point, Adrian
also would have welcomed some overtime because it would
have given him something else to think about besides the
pathetic state of his life. Again, Adrian glanced at the pile
of lonely library books that wouldn't be returned.

He sighed. "No, I'm not busy. What's up?"

"Paul just called me, and he was being really strange.
He didn't have anything important to say, he just told me
that he was at the craft shop getting stuff for school, which
I really didn't care about. But then I heard Celeste's voice

in the background, and I started thinking. Maybe he phoned me so I could phone you and let you know where she is, and what she's doing."

"Uh… Yeah… Thanks…" Adrian let his voice trail off.

Bob mumbled a quick goodbye and hung up. Dial tone buzzed in Adrian's ear.

Adrian turned his head toward the door and hung up the phone.

If it wasn't obvious before that Celeste was avoiding him, it was more than obvious, now.

His chest tightened. He didn't want that. More than anything, he wanted to be with her, to enjoy her laugh and her smile. He wanted to be able to develop their relationship, to be able to show how he felt about her, and to be able to kiss her just because he felt like it, and know that it was okay. But it wasn't just about what he wanted. Right now, everything depended on what Celeste wanted.

Adrian couldn't keep still. He rose, and began to pace. He had to know what she was thinking. He had to know if he still had a chance. And to do that, they had to talk.

As he paced, he glanced into the den. Celeste's sweater lay draped over the back of the chair where she'd left it last time she'd come over to print an assignment for her night-school classes.

He walked into the den, smiled, picked up the sweater then locked up the house.

Before too long, Adrian stepped inside the door of the craft store. Except for the music of a soft-rock radio station playing in the background, the store was quiet. Adrian walked slowly past bins of paint supplies, silk flowers, baskets, wooden pieces and pattern books for every type of craft imaginable, until he found Celeste picking through a bin of colored embroidery thread.

"Hi, Celeste," he said, hoping his voice didn't sound too strained.

Celeste squealed, dropped a couple of skeins on the floor, slapped her hands over her mouth and spun around to face him.

He extended one arm. "I knew you were here, so I brought your sweater that you left at my house. In case you need it."

"My sweater? You came all this way just to return my sweater?"

Adrian shrugged his shoulders. "I…uh…know it's your favorite."

Her eyes narrowed as she studied him, knowing the real reason he was there had nothing to do with returning her sweater. "And how, exactly, did you know I was here?"

He stiffened and cleared his throat. "A little bird told me?"

She turned her head to look down the aisle. "A little bird? I think I smell a rat," she mumbled, not looking at him as she spoke

Adrian shook his head. "Actually, I was talking to Bob, and he mentioned that he'd been talking to Paul and he just happened to hear your voice in the background." He purposely neglected to mention that what he'd just said was exactly the reason for the call, and that nothing else had been discussed.

Her lips tightened.

Before she could say anything, Adrian blurted out the first thing he could think of, just so she wouldn't question him further. "Since we're here, how about if you show me whatever it was that got you interested in cross stitch? You know my mother does cross stitch, so I can at least appreciate it."

Celeste stared at him, knowing that looking at craft supplies had as little to do with him being there as did returning her sweater. "I guess," she mumbled.

They'd just stepped in front of the store owner's masterpiece when Paul appeared beside him with an armful of foam pieces and a bag of colored glitter.

"Adrian? What are you doing here?"

"Celeste forgot her sweater at my place, so I brought it. In case she needs it."

Paul made a short choking sound and coughed. "I was going to take Celeste out for coffee and a donut, but since you're here, why don't you join us?"

Celeste stiffened. "I really don't have time to go out. Maybe I should just go home and you two can go out together."

Paul's eyebrows drew together. "But we came in the same car. Mine."

Adrian raised one finger in the air. "If you've got homework, I can take you home, that way I can help you with it."

Her mouth opened but no sound came out.

Paul smirked. "Or I can go home, and you two can go for coffee. I'm sure Adrian won't mind driving you home."

She responded quickly. "It's okay. I certainly have time to go for out for coffee with you, Paul. I don't know what I was thinking."

Adrian knew exactly what she was thinking—she was trying to avoid him.

He turned to Paul. "Yeah. I'll take you up on that invitation, too. I'd love a donut."

For a split second, Paul hesitated. "Just let me go pay for this."

Celeste held up two small skeins of embroidery thread. "I have to pay, too. I'll go with you."

Adrian followed them both to the cashier's area, and stood to the side as they completed their transactions.

It was no surprise, but Adrian was disappointed that Celeste walked straight for the passenger door of Paul's car instead of his. Paul gave Adrian a sideways glance as he unlocked the door and held it open while Celeste slipped inside, but he said nothing, and they were on their way.

Once they all were seated at the donut shop, conversation and laughter flowed as if things were normal, which Adrian considered both good and bad. After everyone's second cup of coffee, Celeste excused herself to make a trip to the ladies' room.

The second she was out of hearing range, Paul plunked one elbow on the table and turned to him. "I know what you said at basketball, but it really does look like you two had a fight. Are you sure you didn't say something to make her angry?"

"I'm positive," Adrian muttered. "There was no fight."

"Actually, you two aren't exactly in a position to have a fight, because you're not really dating. In fact, have you two ever been on a real date?" Not really expecting an answer, Paul turned his head and watched the entrance to the washrooms. "If she's not going to spend every spare minute with you anymore, I'm still single…" Paul's voice trailed off.

Adrian stiffened involuntarily from head to toe. "Not so fast, my friend," he said between clenched teeth.

Paul let out a whoop of laughter. "Whoa. You've got it bad. I was only teasing you. Here she comes."

Celeste slid into her chair as Adrian forced himself to relax. "It really is time for me to go home, if you don't mind," Celeste said.

Paul shook his head. "Not at all. But I think I have to stop for a short visit at one of the other teacher's homes tonight. Would you mind if Adrian drove you home?"

"I…uh…"

Adrian cleared his throat. "It's okay. I don't mind. I didn't have other plans tonight. Or rather, I did have other plans, but they fell through."

Her cheeks darkened. "Thanks," she mumbled. "I appreciate it."

Paul quickly excused himself and left. Without speaking, Celeste picked up her purse and followed Adrian out to his car in silence.

Adrian did his best to make small talk during the journey home. He didn't want to have a serious discussion when his attention needed to be focused on driving safely. However, while conversation did flow, it was strained.

When he pulled into the driveway, Celeste got out of his car quickly. Completely ignoring the hint, Adrian followed her to her front door and stood beside her while she inserted the key into the lock.

"Are you angry with me?"

The door opened. "No, I'm not angry."

She stepped inside. Adrian followed close behind before she had a chance to close the door with him on the wrong side.

"Have I done something wrong?"

He followed her into the spare bedroom, where she

stored all her embroidery supplies in a box in the corner of the room, since she didn't have any furniture besides the basics. "You've done nothing wrong."

Somehow, her affirmations did nothing to make him feel better about what was happening, or rather, what wasn't happening, between them. "Then why won't you talk to me?"

For a second, her movements froze, then Celeste crouched down and started sorting and packing away her new accessories and colored threads. "It's hard to explain. Before you, I was involved with someone else. We had very different priorities, and at the end, there was a situation I couldn't live with anymore. The way we broke up wasn't very pleasant, so I can't get involved in anything right now."

It made Adrian feel slightly better, even if a twinge of jealousy struck him simultaneously. However, that she was putting the brakes on what was happening because of something someone else had done didn't give him much relief. In fact, it made him feel worse because it trapped him in a situation that was beyond his control. "I'm sorry if it was bad for you, but you've got to realize that I'm not that guy. I think you know where I want this to go. Things would be good between us. If you need time to think about that sort of commitment, I understand."

She dropped the smaller box holding all her threads. "Commitment?"

Adrian stopped and studied Celeste as she stared up at him. To think that whatever they had between them was over was not an option he wanted to consider. Still, he needed more than casual friendship. It was time to raise the bar.

Adrian vowed to himself that he would show Celeste that she could trust him regardless of the other guy's behavior. He hoped she could come to love him the same way he loved her.

Adrian's throat tightened as he realized where his thoughts were going.

Over the last week, his home was empty when Celeste wasn't in it. He loved her, and he wanted her to live with him as his wife. Forever. He wanted all that went with that. Marriage. Kids. A dog. A bird feeder in the backyard. Nosy neighbors. The whole package.

"Yes. Commitment. Let's start by spending more time together and see what happens." Adrian picked up the container, and handed it to Celeste. "I know some guys might think *commitment* is a dirty word, but I don't. I'll let myself out."

Celeste sat at the end of the restaurant table, listening to the other women talk.

She'd weakened. The women she worked with spoke more freely away from the confines of their office building, so Celeste had followed in order to learn from their experiences, so different from her own.

She was the oldest of the junior employees, and definitely the most experienced in some ways of life, but at the same time, completely ignorant in the ways of the dating game. She needed to know how other women carried on a normal relationship, because Celeste's relationship with Zac hadn't been anything near normal. The other women, most of whom ranged from nineteen to twenty-three, compared to her own age of twenty-eight, had plenty of stories about their romantic escapades.

One of them was considering all the things she could do to encourage her boyfriend to pop the question, and was freely discussing all the possibilities with her workmates. Celeste kept silent, but she wanted to tell the woman she'd learned the hard way that giving a man all he wanted wasn't the way to get him to make a commitment.

Commitment.

Adrian's voice echoed through her head.

Zac had said that one day they would get married, but after eight years, she found herself no closer to wedding bells than on the day she moved in with him.

Looking back, Celeste didn't know, on the million-to-one chance that it might have happened, what she would have done if Zac really had asked her to marry him. In the back of her mind she'd always told herself that even if she did marry Zac, she could still leave him anytime. That she hadn't really considered truly committing herself to Zac told her that all along she'd known the situation was less than ideal.

Since she'd been spending so much time with Adrian, she'd begun to see how good a relationship between a man and a woman could be. Beyond the shadow of a doubt, she'd done the right thing in leaving Zac and everything that went with him, in order to make a new start, especially with Adrian showing her the way.

Before meeting Adrian, she couldn't remember the last time she'd laughed just for fun and not at someone's expense. The difference was Adrian in her life. Everything he did was respectable, honest, and honorable.

Until six short months ago, Celeste hadn't been any of those things. She'd laughed at people like Adrian, considering them fools in trying to do the right thing, when there was nothing in it for them.

Somehow, God had broken through her thick skull, and she had discovered that God's ways were right all along. However, she knew nothing of that kind of life, or the people who lived that way. Now that Adrian had dangled the C-word in front of her, knowing that for Adrian, forever really meant forever, the concept scared her to death.

Suddenly, she realized that conversation had stopped, and a couple of the ladies were staring at her.

"Sorry," Celeste muttered as she wiped her mouth with her napkin. "I guess I was thinking about something else. What were you saying?"

Kaitlyn smiled brightly. "I said, since it's payday we're all going to run to the bank before we go back to work. Do you want to come? The waiter was fast today, so we've got extra time. This way we can beat the traffic going home."

Celeste checked her watch. She usually did her banking in her own neighborhood in the evening at the drive-through machine, but if she hadn't missed it, she wanted to hear the end of the story about the time one of the women, Susan, forgot her husband's birthday.

At the thought of birthdays, her stomach clenched and the nice lunch she really couldn't afford threatened to surface.

It would be Adrian's birthday before too long. Not that she expected any sort of romantic date with him—that was exactly what she was trying to avoid. She wasn't the kind of woman Adrian could have a future with. Still, regardless of what she wanted, she loved him deeply. But her background meant she couldn't allow anything more than simple friendship. He was the best friend she had, so she wanted to give him a special present for his birthday, something she'd made herself.

The lady at the craft store had loaned her a pattern that was a personal favorite, then given her a discount on the supplies, so Celeste had been hard at work making Adrian a cover for his computer's mouse which would, she hoped, resemble a real mouse made out of plush, and the cover for the keyboard was supposed to look like a large piece of cheese.

She had started the project before she lost her head and kissed him, but what was done was done. Even if she had to stop seeing him so often, she wouldn't love him any less. In fact, his innocent reaction made her realize just how special he was, and she only loved him more. She would still give him his gift, and then probably turn and run like the coward she was.

"Celeste? Are you okay?"

Celeste cleared her throat and focused her attention back to where it should have been in the first place. "Sorry, I got distracted again. Yes, I need to go to the bank, too."

Celeste walked down the sidewalk in silence, listening to the story of how Susan was planning to cook a special dinner for her husband, then tell him that the reason she forgot his birthday was that she had just discovered she was pregnant.

Celeste nearly stumbled at the news. While all the other women oohed and aahed and congratulated Susan, Celeste stepped back.

Some days Celeste wanted marriage and a baby so badly it hurt, but when she thought about it properly, she knew she couldn't do it. She'd tried to keep a tank of goldfish once. The disgusting process of changing the water far outweighed the joy of watching the fish swimming around. Then they'd all died when she kept forgetting to feed them. In hindsight, even though it was upsetting, it was a good lesson. If she couldn't even keep a few fish alive, she knew she could never care for a baby, regardless of the improvements she'd tried to make in her life.

Still, Celeste was jealous. Which was a sin.

Knowing everyone was concentrating on Susan, while they waited for the light to turn at the crosswalk Celeste briefly closed her eyes and apologized to God for being such a failure.

Fortunately the conversation changed when they entered the bank and took their places in the mercifully short line.

Celeste had just finished her transaction when a familiar voice came from behind her, chilling her to the core of her bones.

"It's been a long time, hasn't it, Celeste?"

She barely choked the words out as she spun around. "Zac… What are you doing here?"

Nothing had changed. He still dressed entirely in black, which was meant to contrast with the highlights of his almost white blond hair. He still wore his jeans so tight she didn't know how he did them up without hurting himself. She noticed that he'd got another piercing, this time his nose, which he had been talking about the last time she'd seen him.

Probably because she'd been away from him for so long, the thing that stood out the most about Zac, besides the earring in his nose, were his glazed, unfocused eyes. Because it was only lunch time, she didn't smell the sickly sweet smell of alcohol on his breath, but the odor of smoke around him nearly gagged her. Anyone nearby would be able to tell he was already high on something.

One corner of his mouth curled up. "I'm doing the same thing that you are. Banking." He glanced down at her purse, then back up to her face. "Although you seem to be doing better than me. After you took off, we had trouble getting bookings. I came downtown to the social services office, telling them I needed money but they wouldn't give it to me. Can you believe they consider me self-employed, and won't give me anything between gigs?"

Celeste knew Zac didn't declare most of his income on his taxes, so he didn't pay for the unemployment insurance he now wanted to collect from. The world didn't owe Zac anything, despite Zac's inflated opinion of his own worth and what he figured he deserved.

She stole a quick glance at the door, where everyone stood waiting for her. Celeste considered this a good thing. Nothing would happen with people watching.

"That's too bad," she muttered. "Now if you'll excuse me, I have to go."

She took one step, meaning to break out into a run the second she cleared the door, but Zac grabbed her arm. "Not so fast. I've been looking for you. Why did you leave me like that?"

"It was all in my note."

She tried to wrench her arm away, but he only tightened his grip. "You didn't give me a chance. I've changed. I want you back."

Between his appearance and his attitude, Celeste could see he hadn't changed. The only thing that had changed was her—she was no longer falling for Zac's lies, or his intimidation. God had helped her discover what was right, and there was nothing right about Zac or the lifestyle she had been leading, so she'd fled. Through God's help and guidance, she was turning her life around before it was too late.

She tried to pull her arm loose. "You're hurting me," she said from between clenched teeth. "Let go. People are watching. I'll scream."

He loosened his grip, but didn't release her. "Don't go. I want to make it up to you."

"You'll never make it up to me. Let me go."

"That's pretty un-Christian of you to say that. After you got religion, didn't you keep telling me that Christians always forgive? You've got to at least listen to what I have to say." Zac pressed his free hand over his heart. "Especially after all we've done together."

Celeste froze. If she hadn't felt like throwing up her lunch before, she felt like it, now. It was just like Zac to rub her face in something, especially when he was right. She probably *was* supposed to forgive Zac, maybe even give him a second chance, even though she knew he was lying about being a changed man. That was Zac's style. He always made promises he never intended to keep, just to get what he wanted.

Because he knew her as well as he did, Celeste could see from Zac's expression the second he knew he'd won this round. His eyes narrowed and he grinned, gloating. "We can get together tonight, since I've got nothing else to do. We'll talk."

She jerked her arm, and this time he released her. "That's too bad, because unlike you, I do have something else to do. If you want to get together we can meet…" Her voice trailed off as she thought about what she'd nearly said. She'd nearly told him that she'd meet him after her night-school classes for that evening.

Just because Zac ran into her at the bank in the middle of the busy downtown core didn't mean he knew anything else about what she was doing with her life. Even if he did find out where she worked, she didn't want him to find out where she attended classes, or, worse, where she lived.

If she were careful, she could meet him a few times, make it plain things were over, and then never see him again.

"We can meet for lunch tomorrow at the taco joint across the street from here."

"Lunch? I was thinking we could go to your new apartment. We can have a few beers and talk."

His words eased her fears, or at least some of them. That he thought she lived in an apartment rather than her humble duplex confirmed that Zac didn't know where she lived. Yet she knew Zac didn't do his banking downtown, so she didn't know if this meeting was just coincidence, or something more. Either way, if she was careful, he would never find her at home. Perhaps if she met him to talk a few times, she could convince him she was never going back to him, or to that kind of life, ever.

"It's lunch, at the taco joint, or nothing. Now if you'll excuse me."

"Okay. Lunch. And you better be there." This time, he let her walk away.

As she joined her workmates and walked back to the office, she realized that Zac would be watching. She almost asked the women deliberately to walk into the wrong building, but if she asked such a thing, she knew the request would only pique their curiosity and invite questions that she didn't want to answer.

She cringed as she walked into her employer's building. He wouldn't know exactly what floor, but now Zac knew her building. She couldn't let him find out where she lived.

Zac was intimately familiar with her car. She didn't know how familiar he was with her mother's car, but she was sure he'd seen it in the course of the years they'd been together. Anyone else she'd known from before, wouldn't be familiar with it, but she couldn't take the chance with Zac. He was devious enough to be watching the exit to the parking lot so he could follow her home. She couldn't let that happen.

Celeste picked up her phone, and dialed Kaitlyn's extension. She tried to sound casual as she spoke. "Kaitlyn? I need a favor. Can you give me a ride to the dry cleaners after work? I'm going to meet someone there, so I'm going to leave my car here in the underground parking overnight and pick it up after work tomorrow."

At Kaitlyn's positive reply, Celeste hung up the phone.

She didn't like being sneaky, but desperate times called for desperate measures. She couldn't tell anyone about the reappearance of Zac into her life. One look at him would reveal everything about the life she'd led not long ago. Everything she didn't want anyone ever to find out. Especially Adrian. The only ones who knew were Pastor Ron and God. And Celeste wanted to keep it that way until she could convince Zac that everything was over, and it was going to stay over, and that he should leave her alone forever. She couldn't risk him hurting her friends.

Now was the time to put into effect everything she'd learned about evasive maneuvers, because she had a feeling she was going to need them.

She could easily take the bus to work in the morning. Zac would never see her because he never got out of bed that early. Her biggest problem would be leaving the building at the end of the day. She could solve that by leaving in someone else's car and bending down to pretend to look for something as they drove out of the exit, where Zac might be waiting for her. But once she was safely away from the underground parking, Celeste had no idea where to go from there. She could take the bus from the dry cleaners to the school, but she would never make it on time for her class in which there was a test tonight. Even if she could be on time taking the bus, she didn't want to be out alone at night, knowing Zac might still be looking for her.

She needed help.

Randy worked at the mall, and he stayed until closing on Tuesdays, which was too late for her to be on time for her class.

Bob ran his auto repair shop, and she knew he had to lock up, so he had to be the last one out. He couldn't leave early.

She'd heard Paul complaining that today was parent-teacher day at the school, and he had meetings until 9:00 p.m.

With a shaking hand, Celeste phoned the only person she had left to ask.

"Hi, Adrian? I hate to do this, but I need a favor…"

Chapter Ten

Adrian watched Celeste drop a pile of books and her purse in front of her on the floor of the car. "Let's go, I'm kind of in a hurry," she mumbled as she fiddled with the pile. As they started moving out of the dry cleaners' parking lot, Celeste hunched her shoulders and looked out the car window, only straightening when they started moving.

"Is that a new coat? I don't remember seeing it before."

"It's not mine. I, uh, had to take my sweater to the dry cleaner, and it was getting cool outside so Kaitlyn loaned me her coat to go home."

Adrian almost started to tease her about her favorite sweater, but stopped himself. Celeste didn't look as if she was in a teasing mood.

He'd been very surprised, first that she'd called him at work, and second, that she'd called him at all, considering the way they'd last parted.

He'd left her home Friday night hoping and praying that all she needed was a little time to think about his declaration that he was ready to take their relationship to the next level.

Sunday at church she'd been pleasant but distant. She hadn't invited him back to her house after the evening service. It hurt, but he told himself that she simply needed more time.

Monday she'd been the same way at the Bible study meeting, not cool, but not overtly friendly, either.

He didn't know what to think of her behavior today. Not that he expected Celeste to fawn and fall all over him. She simply wasn't that way, but he would be a fool if he couldn't tell something was wrong.

He found it very odd to be picking her up from the dry cleaner instead of the office. He knew she was attached to the sweater, so he could almost see her taking it to the dry cleaner immediately after she'd spilled something on it, but nothing explained why she didn't have her car. Unless there was something wrong with the car, too. Whatever was wrong, he wanted to help, although he knew she would never accept money from him, not even a loan. The only thing he could do for her at the moment was to provide transportation.

He reached up and wiggled the knot on his tie. "Is there something wrong with your car?"

She turned to him and smiled weakly. "I haven't got a clue, although I did get another e-mail from my mother. She didn't mention the car, so it must be fine. However, I'm sure there is something seriously wrong with my mother's car, although it isn't running any worse than usual."

A joke. A bad joke, but it was a joke. Adrian chose to take it as a good sign.

"How's your mother doing?"

"Fine. I'm still stunned that after being so happy to retire, she would take a part-time job like that."

"I guess your mother and her sister must be enjoying their time together if they can work together during the day and live in the same house at night."

"I suppose. I'm sure the extra money is nice on top of her pension."

When Celeste's mother had decided to extend her visit, it had been decided that, rather than leave the house empty, her neighbor's adult son would move into the house at a reduced rent in exchange for caring for the lawn and doing normal maintenance until she returned.

Since Celeste was struggling for money, Adrian had suggested that instead she should move into the house, but she had said she wanted to stay in her rented duplex. He didn't understand her decision, but he had purely selfish reasons for doing nothing to attempt to convince her that it was more practical for her to move back into her mother's house. He liked Celeste living where he could always be close to her.

"Did she have any idea when she's coming back?"

"Not really. Since Margie's son is paying rent, that actually gives my mother more motive to stay away. Mom's only expense is to help my auntie pay for the groceries. She's living rent-free, plus she's getting money for renting out her own house and the part-time job. Between having a dependable car for once and living with my auntie, she's having a blast."

It wasn't the way Adrian would want to live, but he realized that different people lived different ways for different reasons.

Adrian pulled up to the drop-off zone in front of the school. "Are you prepared for your test today?"

"Yes. Thanks so much for the ride. I appreciate it."

"How are you getting to work in the morning?"

"I'm not sure. I think I'll just take the bus."

"I have a little bit of work to catch up on. I can leave early and drop you off if you want."

Adrian didn't think the answer would be difficult, but Celeste didn't reply immediately. She unfastened her seatbelt, bent over to pick up her books and her purse, then sat in silence for a few minutes, thinking. "You know, that would work out really well for me. You could even drop me off at the corner, and I'll walk in."

"I could go into the underground parking and let you off from there. I don't mind going a few extra blocks."

She smiled and ran her hand down the front of the borrowed coat. "No, I don't mind walking. I could probably even use the exercise."

Adrian frowned. "Are you sure? I think there's rain in the forecast."

"Really. I don't mind the short walk, even if it does rain." She turned to him and smiled wider. "I don't know where I'd be without you, Adrian. You're really a special guy."

Before he realized what she was doing, Celeste leaned over the stick shift and brushed a kiss on his cheek. "Goodnight. I'll see you in the morning."

She was already out the door before he could collect his thoughts. "Wait! How are you getting home from here?"

"I was just going to take the bus. Or maybe a cab. I have to see how much money I have."

"I can pick you up when classes are over."

"You would do that?"

"Of course." He would do anything for her, especially if it would get them talking again, the way they had before the kiss that shook their world apart.

She glanced from side to side. "As long as it's no trouble."

"No trouble at all. See you later."

Celeste nodded and dashed into the building.

Adrian smiled. He wouldn't push her. He would even stick to neutral topics. When the time was right, Celeste would open up further, but until then, all he could do was be there for her, just as he had been on the first day they'd met. Celeste would see that they were meant to be together.

As soon as the familiar black car appeared around the corner, Celeste pulled up the collar of the raincoat, made sure the strap of the yellow vinyl bonnet was tied firmly beneath her chin, and ran from the shelter of the awning. The second the car pulled into the bus-stop zone she hustled inside. They were mobile so fast she wondered if the car had even come to a complete stop.

She wiped a spray of moisture from her face, not caring that it probably smeared her mascara. She'd never been so thankful for a rainy day.

"Thanks for the ride, Adrian. I really appreciate it."

"No problem. Glad to help."

She waited until they were a block away before removing the wet bonnet, which had hidden her face admirably. She hadn't seen Zac waiting for her, but then she'd run so quickly, she hadn't really had time to look.

But that also meant that Zac wouldn't have been able to look for her, especially since she'd been wearing Debbie's husband's rain gear that Debbie had loaned her since it was still in her car's trunk after his last fishing trip.

Her lunchtime meeting with Zac had gone as expected. As important as Zac had said it was to meet, he was late, and then angry with her when she left before he finished eating, so she could be back to work on time. Of course, he was already angry because she refused to quit her job and go crawling back to him just because he said the band needed her.

For the first time, she hadn't let Zac's anger affect her. After spending most of her time with Adrian, Randy, Bob and Paul, she had learned how normal people behaved, and how good people treated other people. She had learned mutual respect and had seen real friendships in action. She'd seen how friends helped each other, even when there was nothing in it for them.

Zac's reappearance into her life came at exactly the wrong time. For the first time in her life, she was genuinely happy. She was finally moving forward, instead of wallowing in self-pity from day to day. She had given up her dream of being a professional musician, but in doing so, she'd realized an even greater dream, which was having good friends.

Adrian's deep voice broke into her thoughts. "How about getting something at the drive-through, and we can eat at my house. Then we'll have lots of time to relax before the guys get there for practice."

"You're only doing this so you can pay for my meal. I'll only agree if you let me buy the donuts, and don't argue."

He opened his mouth, paused, closed it without speaking, and broke into a grin. "You win. This time. Let's go."

Traffic was heavier than usual due to the inclement weather, so they arrived at Adrian's home later than expected.

"This is bad enough when it's warm," Adrian mumbled after he took his first bite of the take-out burger. "Fortunately, I'm so hungry, I'll eat anything right now."

Celeste nodded, but said nothing as she nibbled on her fries.

Adrian took another bite, chewed it slowly, then laid his burger on the wrapper. "You seem distracted. Do you want to talk about it?"

Celeste looked up in surprise and cleared her throat. She watched Adrian's face. He'd been so kind and so understanding of her changing moods she knew she owed him an explanation, although she didn't know what to say.

It was probably best to tell him the truth, within limitations. "I ran into…an old friend the other day. I guess I've been doing a lot of thinking."

Adrian's face paled. "Would it happen to be the old boyfriend?"

"Actually, yes, it was."

"Oh." He paused and looked down to concentrate on swirling a fry just so into the blob of ketchup. "How did it go?"

"I'm not sure yet. He hasn't changed, that's for sure."

"Do you want him to change?"

Celeste tilted her head, watching Adrian very closely as she spoke. "Yes, of course I do." The more she settled into a good neighborhood and her church, the more she saw what happened when people started to trust God. She wanted the same for Zac, regardless of how she felt about him personally.

Adrian raised his head, cleared his throat, stiffened then

stared into her eyes so intently she forgot to chew. "Do you want to reconcile with him?"

"Reconcile? No. It's over." She never wanted to see Zac again, which was why she had run away and changed her entire life to hide from him. Not only did she not want to see him, Zac actually frightened her.

At first, she'd only been ashamed of the life she'd led. After spending considerable time away from Zac and all he represented, now that she'd seen him again she found him disgusting and creepy, what many people she now knew would have called a 'low-life.' Not long ago, she was no different. More than ever, she didn't want Adrian to know the lifestyle she'd been living when she was with Zac. She didn't want Adrian to consider that side of her, it disgusted her so much.

"I think you know how I feel about you. Knowing it's officially over between you and your previous boyfriend, I'd like to make it official and take you out for dinner, to someplace nice. I'm talking about the kind of place I've been wanting to take you for a long time, and you would never go. I think the usual line is for me to say we should get to know each other better, but that's so overused. Consider this an opportunity to talk, away from other distractions. How about it?"

"I don't know. What you're talking about sounds like you're asking me out on a date."

"What if I am?"

"I don't know."

Adrian leaned back, crossed his arms and quirked one eyebrow. "If you don't say you'll go, then you'll force me to act like Randy and beg you."

Celeste instantly remembered the day Adrian was re-
ferring to. It was the first time she'd met Randy, and he
had begged her to stay and play one song with them. That
day was the catalyst to her joining the worship team. That
one day had changed her life more than Adrian would
ever know.

"I—"

Her words were cut off by the sound of the doorbell, followed by the sound of someone coming in the front door
without waiting for an answer.

"Man, it's pouring out there. Hey, I smell food! Adrian?
Where are you?"

Celeste bit back a giggle. "Speaking of Randy…"

Adrian pushed his half eaten burger to the center of the
table and stood. "I'm in the kitchen!" he called out to
Randy, then lowered his voice as he turned to Celeste and
quickly checked his watch. "I haven't even started the coffee yet. What's your answer?"

Celeste glanced to the doorway, knowing Randy would
be there in seconds.

She gulped. "Yes," she muttered, not knowing if she was
doing the right thing, but she didn't know what else to do.

Randy appeared in the doorway. "Where's the donuts?
You guys didn't eat them all, did you?"

Celeste covered her half-eaten burger with the wrapper,
and tucked it into the fridge. "Didn't have time. Let's get
everything set up while Adrian makes the coffee. Paul and
Bob will be here any minute."

Immediately upon entering the den, Celeste and Randy
sorted through the patch cords and started to plug everything in.

"I didn't see your car in the driveway. How did you get here? You didn't walk on a day like this, did you?"

"I left the car at work. Adrian gave me a ride."

Randy froze, one of the jacks in his hand, aimed at the input plug-in. "What's wrong with your car?"

She couldn't tell Randy she'd been leaving the car in the underground parking at work so Zac wouldn't see it and follow her home.

Celeste shrugged her shoulders, trying to appear casual as she spoke. "Nothing more than usual, I guess. I just thought it best to leave the car at work and hitch a ride."

"Oh. Do you need a ride home tonight?"

"Sure. That would be great."

Celeste resumed helping Randy set everything up.

For today, she was safe from Zac, but with the recent turn of events, would her heart ever be safe from Adrian?

Bob Delanio could no longer see the receptionist after she disappeared around the corner, but he could hear her.

"Celeste, there's a man here to see you."

He recognized Celeste's voice when she replied, but he couldn't make out her words. The receptionist's reply sounded loud and clear.

"No, he didn't give his name."

Again, Celeste said something he couldn't make out.

Bob knew Celeste wasn't expecting him, but he hadn't expected that she wouldn't want to see him.

The receptionist's voice sounded loud and clear, lacking any semblance of trying to be discreet. "No, he's not blond—he's got dark hair. No earrings or jewelry of any kind. If it helps, I think he's your mechanic."

This time, he could hear Celeste's voice quite plainly. "Mechanic? I don't have a mechanic."

"But he asked for you specifically. He's got a big smear of something black on his face, and he's wearing gray coveralls." Her voice lowered, but not by much. "There's a crest on them that says "Bob and Bart's.""

Bob quickly pulled a rag out of his pocket and wiped at his cheek, hoping he was wiping the right one. Not knowing whether or not he'd gotten rid of the axle grease, he shoved the rag back in his pocket when the click of heels on the tile floor approached from around the corner.

"Bob? What are you doing here?"

"Randy told me you had to leave your car here for a few days, so I started thinking. There are a number of minor adjustments I could make. I know about a few things that are about to go, and I managed to find the parts at a wrecker's, so. . ." He shrugged his shoulders. "I called Adrian and told him I'd pick you up today, and I'll have a look at it."

Her cheeks turned a cute shade of pink. "Oh, Bob, you really didn't have to go to all this trouble. I can still drive it, I just chose not to."

"I know, but it's better to be safe than sorry. That thing really isn't in the best condition, and I haven't looked at it for a while. I hope you're remembering to check your oil once a week."

She nodded. "Yes, I am. I feel bad that you came all the way downtown for nothing."

"One of my sisters is thinking of buying a used car, and I don't like any of my family to buy anything without me looking at it first. So I wasn't far away. It's not a big deal. It really would make me feel better if I had a look at it."

She glanced over her shoulder, but he couldn't see her desk from where they stood. "I'll be finished work in about ten minutes. Would you mind hanging out here for a bit?"

"Actually, I parked my own car in the underground parking, and I couldn't help but see yours. If you'll give me the keys, I can start now."

The entire time they were talking, the receptionist had been watching them, making no attempt to hide her interest. The second Celeste returned to her desk to retrieve her keys, the receptionist leaned forward, smiled and folded her hands on the desk in front of her. "Do you often make house calls?"

Bob smiled. "No. Only for family and good friends." He reached into his pocket, withdrew a business card, and handed it to her. "But if you're ever in the neighborhood and need some work done, we'd be happy to help you."

Before he could give his customary spiel on guarantees and customer satisfaction, Celeste appeared with the keys. "Great, I'll see you down there."

He had the impression the receptionist wanted to chat, but Bob didn't have the time, nor did he have any interest in flirting when he had a job to do. He returned to the underground parking to check Celeste's mother's car.

At two minutes past the half hour, people began flowing through the underground parking facility, as those who worked in the building ended their work day. Celeste soon appeared beside him.

"Find anything?"

Bob straightened and swiped his hands on his pants. "Yeah, I did. The engine is out of time, which means the alignment between the spark plugs and the pistons isn't right."

"Is that bad?"

"Not initially, but when I took the distributor apart I saw that the whole thing has to be replaced. That's only the start of it. I want to take it back to the shop. You can take my car to night school."

"Are you sure? If there really isn't anything more wrong than usual, I can still drive it. It's okay, really."

Bob frowned. The only thing okay with the car was that the headlights were properly aimed. All the guys knew the deplorable condition of Celeste's mother's car, but she would never allow him to do any serious work on it. The only exception had been one Saturday when they'd all found themselves congregating at Celeste's duplex. Still, he hadn't been able to do much in her driveway.

Replacing the distributor was minor. He knew from the consistent spots on the street where she parked that the car was leaking oil. He wanted to put the car up on the hoist to investigate further.

Celeste refused to let him do the work for free, but she didn't have the money to do everything needed, so nothing was done. When Bob heard she'd left the car at work, the situation presented the perfect opportunity to get his hands on it while it was down. He'd phoned Adrian and told him not to pick Celeste up, because he was going to get the car back to his shop, even if he had to call a tow truck to do it. Finally he could really get to fixing it. Or at least get to what could be done until she arrived after work on Friday to pick it up.

Adrian had expressed his relief that finally something was going to be done about the car, but in the process, Bob had one of the very few arguments he'd ever had with

Adrian. Adrian had offered to pay for the parts, and even pay him for his labor. While Bob could understand Adrian's impulse, Bob had been incredibly insulted. He had no intention of letting Celeste pay for the parts, and he certainly wasn't going to charge for his time to fix the car. He certainly wouldn't have accepted the money from Adrian for what he intended to do for Celeste for free. He liked Celeste too, and he knew she needed the help. Regardless of what she said, he intended to cover the cost of the parts himself, without any help from Adrian.

Bob had been stunned to find himself arguing with his friend until he realized the reason for the argument. While he simply wanted to help a friend, Adrian's concern went far further than friendship. Adrian's voice changed when he started talking about Celeste. The guys would be talking about something else, and the usually focused Adrian would get distracted, and somehow, Celeste's name would come into the conversation. That would be on the few times they even saw Adrian anymore, because he was spending almost all his time with Celeste.

Adrian had it bad.

Bob continued, "I've never been comfortable with you driving that car in this condition. Humor me."

Her smile dropped, and she stepped back. Finally she could see he meant business.

"Uh, thanks. I really appreciate this. My mother probably won't recognize her car by the time she gets it back."

"I hope that's the case. Let's go before the traffic gets any worse. I want to listen to it as it drives, so you can drive my car home."

The entire drive back to the shop, Bob made mental

notes about all the hums, clunks and other assorted sounds. He pulled the car directly into one of the open service bays, and met Celeste in the lobby.

He stepped behind the counter and filled out a key tag, making a specific note to Bart, his partner, not to touch it, that Bob wanted to do all the work himself. "I might go to bed early tonight," he said as he wrote. "So take my car to work tomorrow and I'll get it from you either Friday night, or on the weekend."

"But what will you do for transportation?"

Bob relaxed, and broke out into a broad grin. "You don't think that car is the only thing I have to drive, do you? For fun, I've got my baby tucked away. This just gives me a good opportunity to uncover her."

"Should I ask?"

Bob's grin widened. "Probably not. Now get going before you're late for night school. I'll see you here on Friday."

Chapter Eleven

Adrian bit his lip to keep from laughing at the lift of Celeste's eyebrows as soon as she opened the menu.

"Do you see these prices? What in the world were you thinking?"

He cleared his throat and tried to keep a straight face. He'd never had a date complain about the amount he intended to spend, but then, Celeste had been bucking him every step of the way, refusing to call it a date, even though it was. "I told you it's my treat. Ignore the prices. Order whatever you want."

"What if I feel like a lobster?"

"That's funny. You don't look like a lobster."

She met his joke with a stony stare.

Adrian couldn't hold back his laughter. "Lighten up, Celeste. It's going to be fun to wine and dine you. Minus the wine."

She lowered her menu to the table. "Why?"

Adrian also lowered his menu. "What do you mean?"

"Why did you pick a place like this? By the time the

final bill comes, you'll have spent more on one meal than I spend on an entire week's worth of groceries."

He had so much he wanted to say, he didn't know where to start. "That's not the point. I wanted to take you somewhere special, where we could talk."

She turned her head, taking in the soft lighting, accented by a colored candle at each table. Soft, soothing music echoed in the background. The elegant decorating was clearly geared toward romance and not family dining. The well-spaced tables were mostly occupied by couples who were obviously on dates.

"We could have talked over a burger, just the same."

"No, we couldn't have. This place is quiet and private. Relax."

Celeste once more raised the menu, but he could see from her eyes that she wasn't reading. She was studying everything around her. Abruptly, it dawned on him that she might never have been to a place like this. If so, he could understand why she would have found the prices intimidating.

Her attention returned to the menu, but Adrian knew it was pointless. She would order the second least expensive item, whether she liked it or not, just so he couldn't accuse her of ordering the cheapest thing on the menu.

"I hope you're hungry. And I want you to order something you like. Maybe something you've never had before. The food here is excellent."

Her voice was so low he barely heard her reply. "Are you sure this is okay?"

"If it wasn't okay, I wouldn't have brought you here."

"You only brought me here because Bob still has my car. Or my mother's car. The car I've been driving for the past six months." Celeste covered her face with her hands. "I'm babbling. I must sound like an idiot. Can you tell I'm nervous?"

"It's okay. You'll get over it as soon as you start eating."

She raised her head. "I still don't understand why you brought me to a place like this."

"I think it should be obvious by now, Celeste."

Celeste's beautiful jade-green eyes widened. Eyes a man could get lost in. Eyes that showed wonder and inner joy, yet still reflected struggles. Struggles that he wanted to share with her, but she wouldn't let him.

"I just hope that by coming, I'm not making a promise to you I can't keep."

All Adrian's carefully rehearsed words about love and discussing future plans deserted him. "Of course not," he said. "I wanted to get away from everything else and just talk."

She smiled weakly. "Well, I guess we couldn't talk at the library tonight, could we? That wouldn't be allowed. Besides, by the time we're finished here, the library will be closed."

"Probably."

"When do you think we'll go? I need something new, because I've finished everything in the last pile." Her cheeks darkened. "We missed going to the library last week."

Adrian folded his hands on the table in front of him. While it was good that she had finally admitted in a roundabout way that she'd been avoiding him, it wasn't the reason he wanted to take her out for dinner. He also hadn't brought her to a place like this to discuss going to the library. "If you want we can go tomorrow."

"Great. I'd like that. Besides, I know how you hate to pay overdue fines. You probably have to go, too, don't you?"

The waiter appeared to take their orders, which was a good distraction. However, after the waiter left, instead of talking about what he wanted, they talked about the same kind of things they always talked about, including the nice turn in the weather. By the time the waiter came with their meals, the conversation had drifted to the latest books they'd read, which in turn brought the topic of conversation back to the library.

Adrian tried not to grimace. Celeste, however, caught him, and broke out into a grin. "Can I help it if I like going to the library? Just one of these times, I'd like to pick you up instead of always going in your car. Tomorrow would be a good day for that, since I'll still have Bob's car." She started to grin, then bit her lower lip until she had herself under control. "I know how you feel about my mother's car." Her expression once again became serious. "Do you have any idea what Bob is doing with it? He said he ordered some kind of part, and he was going to give it back to me tonight, which obviously didn't happen."

"I don't know. You'll have to ask him."

"But he's being so evasive. I have a bad feeling he's doing a lot of extra work he's not telling me about. I feel funny about it, because his time is expensive. He said all he wants me to pay for is the used parts from the wrecker. That's not fair."

"He started the shop with Bart because he likes fixing cars, so it's kind of like a hobby that developed into a career. It's probably not often that someone brings in such a, um…classic…for him to work on. Maybe he really is having fun with it. After all, it's what Bob likes to do best."

"I don't know about that. Is it possible to have fun on the job? I enjoy my job, but I wouldn't call it fun."

Adrian grinned. "I think that depends. I know Randy has fun at his job, but then we all know what Randy can be like."

Celeste grinned back. "I know what you mean. Do you remember the day we bought my computer? He was being so creative piling up those remote control trucks. I bet he was playing with the demo model before he started cleaning up. I wonder—what is his apartment like?"

"It's untidy, but somehow Randy knows where everything is. And he has almost every electronic gadget known to man." He also knew that Randy spent a lot of time at work playing computer games when there wasn't anyone in the store.

"That shouldn't surprise me. I had to laugh when I saw him trying to take pictures of Paul with the camera in his cell phone. He was driving Paul nuts, which says a lot, because Paul is always so patient, working with kids every day. He seems to love his job too."

"I don't know. I've never really talked to him about it." Adrian tried to keep the exasperation out of his voice, but failed. "I didn't bring you here to talk about the other guys. I wanted to talk about us."

Celeste hunched her shoulders. "There is no 'us.'"

Adrian leaned forward and lowered his voice. "I think there is, and you know it," he muttered. "It's time to acknowledge it. I want to get to know you better. Have fun."

She grimaced fleetingly at his words, then cleared her throat. "But we've been having fun."

"That's true, but we don't ever go anyplace except for the library. Aside from that, everything we do is either church-related or we go to each other's homes."

"We sometimes do our grocery shopping together."

Adrian resisted the urge to drag his hand over his face. "That doesn't count. I'm talking about going out and doing regular, normal things, like couples do when they're…" Adrian's sentence stalled. Celeste's face paled, stopping him from saying the words on the tip of his tongue, which were *in love*. He cleared his throat, and thought of an emergency substitution. "…like when they're dating. How about if we start with a movie?"

Her face brightened. "That's great. The video store's got a special on this month. If you rent a new release, you get a seven-day rental for free."

Adrian shut his eyes in frustration. "I'm not talking about renting a movie. I'm talking about a real movie. Like going to a theater. With an oversized watered-down soda and cold popcorn with too much artificial butter."

"Wow. You make that sound so appealing."

The waiter reappeared with their meals, Adrian said a short prayer of thanks, and they began to eat.

Celeste's eyebrows arched at her first bite, she paused, smiled, then quickly speared another piece of salmon. "This is fabulous!"

"I told you it would be."

Adrian had never seen Celeste talk so little while she ate, but he took that to be a sign that she was enjoying the meal. He chose to say little and just let her eat in peace.

After her plate was empty, Celeste set her fork down and lightly patted her mouth with her napkin. "That was so good! Thank you. I know you said the cheesecake here was spectacular, but I'm too full for dessert. Should we think about heading home?"

Adrian's breath caught. He wanted to take her home, but

not to her home. He wanted to take her to his home, except that instead of it being just *his* home, he wanted it to be *their* home.

His heart started beating in double time. If they were married, they would be going home together. It didn't matter if they read, watched television, talked, or even if they didn't talk. They would still be together, and that was all that mattered.

"I have an idea. Since we didn't have dessert, why don't you come over to my place? By that time, maybe we'll be feeling like dessert, and we can dip into that Rocky Road ice cream I bought last time we went grocery shopping together. As well, we could have more coffee, and that would keep us both awake."

Celeste blinked. "More coffee? You're kidding, right? I think I'm past the point of no return here. I've been drinking coffee all day, and now I've had more. I'm still sleepy, but all that coffee has had another effect on me. I had better pass for tonight, but before that…" She stood. "I'll be right back," she said, and headed in the direction of the ladies' room.

As soon as she disappeared, Adrian took advantage of her absence to signal the waiter and quickly paid the bill, so he wouldn't have to listen to Celeste try to make a contribution when he knew she couldn't afford it. When he had mentioned the ice cream, he had seen a spark of interest, which made him suspect that the reason she had passed on dessert was the price.

When Celeste returned, Adrian led her outside, but instead of taking her to her car, he led her to the curb and pointed down the hill to the sunset.

"How would you like to stand here for a while and watch?"

Celeste hadn't buttoned her jacket; she'd only slipped it on for the short walk to the car. Now, even though they intended to stay outside for a few minutes, she still left the buttons undone, only pulling the two sides together just under the collar, bunching it in her fist to hold it semi-closed. "That would be nice. It's so pretty."

She turned to watch the hues of pink and purple melding together, but while Celeste watched the sky, Adrian watched Celeste.

He wanted her to trust him, to open her heart and soul and share whatever it was that held her back from deepening their relationship. He was ready to commit himself to her, if only she would accept him.

Tonight, after their first real date, was a good time to start. At this moment, with the beauty of the sunset in front of them, the setting was perfect.

A cool breeze drifted across the expanse of the parking lot, causing Celeste to shiver. Adrian took advantage of the opportunity and stepped closer to her. Only her eyes moved to acknowledge the change, so he took that as a sign of encouragement. Slowly, he wrapped one arm around her and drew her close to him, both to shelter her from the wind, and also to keep her warm.

She started to lean into him, and Adrian considered that a good thing. But then, when she realized what she was doing, she stiffened.

He didn't want to let her go, but he didn't want to force her to stay.

Adrian let his arm drop.

She turned her head and stared at him. "What are you doing?"

Adrian raised his arm in an automatic reaction to straighten his tie, even though he wasn't wearing one. He tugged at his collar, then rammed his hands into his coat pockets. "I was trying to be romantic. If you have to ask, then I must assume I'm doing something wrong."

"I…." her voice trailed off. She cleared her throat, then turned her head and stared off into the sunset. "You're not doing it wrong. It's just that it's been so long since anyone's been romantic to me, I don't know what to do anymore."

"But… I thought you just recently split up with someone. Surely…"

She shook her head and abruptly crossed her arms over her chest. "No. We never did anything so simple as watch sunsets. I actually haven't done much sunset-watching at all."

"Then maybe it's about time you started."

"Maybe, but I should be watching sunsets alone. I don't want to spoil things."

Adrian blinked. "Spoil things? I don't understand."

She kept her face pointed at the fading sunset. "I already told you. Getting romantic will spoil our friendship. I don't want that to happen."

"But…" Adrian let his voice trail off. As far as he was concerned, their 'friendship' had already been spoiled. They had progressed beyond what he termed *friendship* with a kiss that had rocked his world off its axis. For as long as he lived, he would never forget that night, or the way she'd kissed him. He also would never forget how he'd felt when he'd kissed her and she had responded. It couldn't be taken back. It had happened. If she had just passed it off casually, he could have accepted that she didn't take the power of the moment as seriously as he did. But, her strong reaction and her actions afterward told him that she'd been as affected by the moment and all its ramifications as he was.

"You're wrong. I think our friendship will be spoiled if you keep avoiding me."

"I'm not avoiding you. I'm here with you now, aren't I? We're going to the library tomorrow, aren't we?"

Adrian sighed. Again, they were back to the library. Where all couples went to spend a romantic, fun-filled Friday night. He gave his head a small shake at the concept. "That's not what I meant. Why don't you want to try being more than just friends with me?"

"Because it's not meant to happen. It would never work between us. So let's just keep things as they are, okay?"

He sucked his lower lip between his teeth. He wanted to tell Celeste that he loved her, and it could work, but he held his tongue. For now, if she was convinced it couldn't work, anything he said or did would only strengthen her resolve and make the situation worse. Instead, all he could do was move slowly. He would prove to her that he could be trusted, and that he would be there for her. Always, and for everything.

"Okay, I won't argue with you. Are we still on for ice cream? If you don't want any more coffee, I can make that tea you like."

Her eyes brightened, and strange things happened to his stomach, even though he knew he was far from hungry. "Yes. I'd like that. Let's go."

Chapter Twelve

Celeste rolled onto her back and stared up at the dark ceiling. The only things keeping the room from total blackness were the green glow of the numbers on the clock radio, and what little light seeped through the heavy curtains from the streetlamps two houses down.

She should have been sleeping, but as tired as she was, she couldn't.

When she'd finally got home, there was a message from Bob on her answering machine. The car was ready, and he quoted a ridiculously cheap price on the parts he'd used. Bob said to come and get it any time, which would be no problem, because she still had his car.

If the inability to adequately repay a debt wasn't bad enough, Adrian had heard the message, and had offered to loan her the money if she didn't have it.

Adrian.

Celeste squeezed her eyes shut, even though in the dark there was nothing to blank out.

In stark contrast to everything that made Adrian the

man he was, there was Zac, the personification of everything bad she'd ever done, returning to haunt her. He had
refused to accept how much she'd changed, so she'd agreed
to meet Zac one more time, which she'd done earlier that
day at the taco restaurant downtown during her lunch
break. This time, Zac had been on time, and, even though
he still always had a cigarette burning, he was coherent.
However, his one day of good behavior didn't change her
mind. Again, she'd told him that everything was over and
that she never wanted to see him again. Ever. This time,
he'd been strangely silent and not argued with her. When
he'd left, she could tell he was mad, but he did go away,
and this time, he didn't threaten her. She could only take
that to mean he'd finally accepted that nothing he could do
or say would change her mind. It really was over between
them. For good.

Even after all their years together, Celeste had no regrets
about leaving Zac. Yet, the fact of him being gone didn't
erase that part of her life and everything going with it that
Zac represented. Nothing in her life during those years
had been good or pleasing to God. Even before she accepted Jesus into her heart, she knew she wasn't living a
good life. She couldn't even use love as an excuse. Now
that she knew what real love was like, she knew she never
had loved Zac. She'd stayed with him and gone along with
his decadent lifestyle because it was the easiest thing to do.

She rolled over and buried her face in her pillow. She
loved Adrian, who did live a life that was good and pleasing
to God, but she wasn't pleasing enough to God to have him.

Outside, the neighbor's dog barked. She listened for
her landlord's dog to start barking from the other side of

the duplex, then remembered that Hank had asked her to take in the newspaper, meaning he and his family, including the dog, had gone away for the weekend.

She rolled over again, and pulled the blanket up to her chin. Without the sound of Hank's children playing their loud computer games from the other side of the wall, she could sleep in for once on a Saturday morning.

If she could get to sleep. Tomorrow, she was going to the library with Adrian. She knew he didn't understand why she enjoyed going to the library so much, and she doubted he ever would. No one in their right mind could call weekly trips to the library a date, but in going, she spent hours with the man she truly loved, with no strings attached. Neither of them put on airs, no one had to pretend to be something they were not. The library was quiet, relaxed and anonymous, and therefore, perfect.

The neighbor's dog barked again, louder this time. The woman yelled at the dog to get inside, and once again, all was silent.

Then the doorbell rang.

Celeste sat up in bed with a start. The glow from the clock radio read 2:49 a.m.

The doorbell rang a second time.

Celeste's heart pounded. She didn't know if she should ignore it and hope the person went away, or if she should answer, in case it was someone who was in trouble and needed help.

But she was alone. She wasn't going to open the door, not for any person, not for any reason.

For an irrational second, she considered barking like a

dog, except that if she really did have a dog, the dog would have barked long ago.

She sucked in a deep breath, crept out of bed, and tip-toed out of the bedroom until she was at the top of the stairs. Up until recently, she had considered the layout of the duplex a nuisance, with the kitchen, living room and bathroom downstairs, and the two bedrooms upstairs. Now, she was grateful for the distance from the door.

Visible through the colored glass beside the door, a dark figure moved outside. The person's height put them close to the top of the window, which meant it probably was a man.

The doorknob rattled as the man tested it to see if it was locked.

Celeste's heart stopped briefly. She quickly praised God that every night the last thing she did before going to bed was check the front door to make sure it was securely locked.

She had started to turn around to go back to the bedroom to call the police when a deep voice, muffled through the glass, sounded from outside. "I know you're there. Let me in, Celeste. We need to talk."

Celeste froze midstep.

Zac.

He'd discovered where she lived. She thought she'd been careful.

The doorknob rattled again, only this time more violently. "I said, let me in!"

"Go away or I'll call the police!" she called out, walking to the very edge of the first step.

Zac pounded his fist on the door three times. "Do that, and you'll be sorry."

Celeste forced herself to breathe. Zac had been in many

altercations where the police were called. Not long before she'd left him, he'd been involved in a fight that was so bad she'd had to bail him out when she sobered up enough to drive. The other man had been taken to the hospital. She had no doubt that in Zac's present state, he would do the same, if not worse, to her.

"I said go away!" she forced herself to yell back.

"Are you trying to hide that other guy? The one who answered the phone? He can't protect you." The door shook, banging so violently she didn't know how the doorknob didn't come off. A long string of very nasty words followed.

She began to tremble from head to foot. In Zac's present state, Adrian was no match for Zac. Once when Zac had flipped out, she'd seen him take down three men, all larger than himself.

"I'm not opening the door! Go away!"

"You'd better open up, Celeste! We have to straighten some things out. You owe me!"

Celeste's stomach rolled. She owed him nothing. He owed *her,* in wages and the possessions she'd had to leave behind, to say nothing of her savings that he'd stolen. But she knew Zac didn't see it that way, or he wouldn't have been pounding on her door in the middle of the night.

"Go away! I said I'll call the police!"

Instead of a reply, something hard hit the glass.

Celeste turned and ran back into the bedroom. At the same second as her fingers hit the last digit of 911, the crash of breaking glass echoed through the otherwise silent house.

She dropped the phone receiver on the floor. By the time someone answered, Zac would be upstairs. By the time the police actually arrived, it would be too late. He would have her.

Celeste ran to the bedroom door and closed it, but realized it had no lock.

She'd seen in movies where people braced a chair under the doorknob to keep someone out. Not only did she not know exactly what to do, she didn't have a chair in the bedroom. But even if she did, in his present state, Zac would break through a hollow-framed interior door in seconds.

The front door creaked.

Footsteps crunched through the broken glass.

"No…" she whimpered.

Hank wasn't home. It would do no good to scream.

She had nowhere to go. She couldn't run down the stairs to go outside. Zac would already be on his way up. She couldn't take the chance that he would search for her downstairs first. The bedrooms were always upstairs. Besides, the closed door was a dead giveaway to where she was. *Dead* being the key word. If he didn't merely rape her, in Zac's current state of rage, Zac just might kill her, too.

She backed up. With the door closed, the room was darker than ever. The green glow from the clock radio suddenly became eerie. Even the filtered light from the window felt ominous.

The window…

Celeste ran to the window. She couldn't jump from the second story without breaking any bones, but Hank's apple tree was right outside the window, Hank's *sturdy tall* apple tree.

It should hold the weight of a full-grown person.

Celeste fumbled with the latch, hiked the window open, and stuck one leg out. The cool night air assaulted her bare toes, but the cold was a far lesser evil than what awaited her if she stayed.

She reached forward as far as she could, leaned toward the tree, said a quick prayer for mercy, and launched herself at the large branch that only a month before, she had picked apples from, using a long-handled fishing net she'd borrowed from Randy.

Ignoring the painful scrapes from the branches, Celeste hung on tight for a few seconds while she gained some balance, then started to shimmy down the tree. A foul string of nasty words blasted the night air as Zac entered the bedroom to discover she wasn't there. Only halfway down the tree trunk, Celeste froze. She didn't know how stoned Zac was, but she only had a chance of escape if he didn't realize the window was open behind the curtains. If he did look, she had to remain still. Hopefully he wouldn't see her if she stayed melded into the tree, still only halfway to the ground. Most of all, if Zac was listening, if she moved he would hear the smaller branches snapping, even though she tried her best to be quiet.

When the swearing became quieter and it sounded as if he had left the bedroom and started looking through the rest of the house for her, Celeste continued downward. The second her bare feet touched the cold, wet grass, she broke into a full run.

She didn't think about where she was going. Instinct told her where she would be safe.

She ran with every ounce of strength she had.

Gasping so hard it hurt, Celeste banged on the door with the last bit of energy she had left. "Adrian! Let me in! Please! Let me in!"

Even though her hands stung from the slashes of the branches, after fifteen seconds had passed, she grabbed the doorknob with both hands and frantically started alternately pushing, pulling and turning it.

Tears burned her eyes as she gulped for air. "Adrian! Help me!"

The porchlight flashed on, the sudden light stinging her eyes. The doorknob turned beneath her hands. Celeste blinked in the bright light and released the doorknob as if it were on fire.

The door opened. Adrian stood in the doorway. He was barefoot, wearing only crumpled jeans with the button unfastened. His usually meticulously styled hair stood on end. For the first time since she'd known him, he wasn't wearing his glasses, so he was squinting rather badly.

He was the most beautiful thing she'd ever seen.

"Celeste?" His eyes narrowed even more as he focused on the brightness of pink flannel. "What are you doing here in your pajamas? Where's Bob's car?" He glanced over her shoulder to the empty street. Seeing nothing, he then looked down and stared at her bare toes. "You'd better come in."

The second the door closed behind her, she extended one arm and pointed in the direction of her duplex. "It's Zac," she gasped. She was trembling from head to toe, but she gulped for more air, and continued. "He found me. He's at my house. I had to run."

"Who's Zac? Should I call the police?"

Celeste inhaled deeply a few times, finally gaining control of her breathing, and shook her head. "There's no point. He'll be gone by now. As soon as he realizes I'm not there, he'll check the obvious places in the yard and then leave within three minutes."

"Three minutes?"

"He always times everything to three minutes so the police won't catch him. Because he was looking for me first, I don't know if he had time to steal anything." For a second, her heart stopped again. She didn't have much worth stealing. All she had besides some used furniture was her economy CD player, the television she'd got from the second-hand store and her reconditioned computer, none of which Zac would want. They weren't worth enough to bother stealing because they weren't name-brand items and they would be hard to sell because they were older.

The thing he would want would be her electric piano, because it was the only thing she owned of any value. Fortunately, the piano was still set up in Adrian's den, where she'd left it after practice on Wednesday.

Celeste's relief quickly changed to dread. With nothing to steal, and without her there for him to have his way with, Zac could trash the place.

Her home.

She hoped his three minutes would be up before he had time to vent his rage.

"I don't understand. Why would someone you know steal your things? If you knew he was going to steal something, why did you let him in?"

Celeste lowered her arm and turned her head so she could see Adrian's face. His obvious confusion told her that he had no experience with the dark side of people beyond what he saw on television or read in the paper. But she knew that kind of person well. Not long ago, she'd been one of them.

"I didn't let him in. He broke in. That's why I'm here."

"But…" Adrian shook his head. "Just a minute. This is all wrong. I'll be right back."

He returned wearing his glasses and a T-shirt. The button on his jeans was fastened, but he was still barefoot. Draped over his arm, he carried a large bathrobe, which he handed to her as soon as he was within reach. "Put this on and tell me what's going on."

He glanced at the window, even though it wasn't possible to see anything, then back to her, waiting for an explanation.

She didn't know what to say, but standing in Adrian's foyer in the middle of the night, dressed only in her pajamas and now Adrian's bathrobe, she owed him some kind of explanation.

The time had come to tell Adrian everything.

The truth had never been so difficult. Telling Pastor Ron had been almost…business. Telling Adrian was personal. Very personal. It was also very different now that Zac had found her.

"I'm so cold. May I have some tea?"

"Tea?" He glanced again in the direction of her home, then focused his attention back to her. "I suppose."

She followed Adrian to the kitchen and watched from the doorway while he ran the water and started to fill the kettle.

Telling him would be easier if she didn't have to face him.

She spoke while his back was still turned. "Zac got rather upset when I disappeared so abruptly."

He didn't look at her as he continued to fill the kettle. "Go on."

Celeste sucked in a deep breath and wrapped her arms

around herself. It was time to trust God, fully, that she could say the truth and leave it in God's hands.

She didn't know if she was ready, but she no longer had any options.

"I know you've wondered about how easily I could play in front of people when I joined the worship team. The truth is that I've been in a band before."

Adrian turned off the tap and set the kettle on the stove. He spoke with his back still turned as he turned the stove on. "You already told me that. You said the band broke up."

Celeste cringed. When she'd said that she'd purposely left out most of the details. Today she couldn't. "That's not really the whole story. What really broke up was me and Zac. I more or less ran away. One day when he wasn't home, I took my clothes, a few personal things, my piano, my car, and I left him."

Adrian turned around. His eyes were wide, and his face had paled. "You're married?!"

Celeste gulped. "No, we weren't married." She let him draw his own conclusions. Judging from his horrified expression, he was drawing the right ones.

He cleared his throat. "I see," he mumbled as he reached into the cupboard for the box of tea. "Were you not happy?"

Not happy didn't begin to cover how she'd felt in the months leading up to her parting from Zac.

"It wasn't just Zac. It was also the lifestyle. I tried talking to Zac, but he wouldn't listen. I couldn't survive in those surroundings any more, and that's why I left."

Adrian's eyebrows arched, and his expression went blank. Celeste could see things were getting worse instead of better. He couldn't have understood why she left the way she did, if he didn't know the full story.

The kettle whistled.

Adrian turned around to fill the teapot.

It was easier talking to him when he was busy, and not looking at her.

"You know when you go to a bar, where the crowd is drunk and loud and obnoxious, most of people in the building are stoned, and the band isn't in much better condition than the people in the chairs?"

Adrian turned around. He crossed his arms over his chest and tilted his head slightly to one side.

"I can't say that I do."

Celeste gulped. Of course he wouldn't know. He'd likely never been in such a place in his life. On the other hand, Celeste had been to almost every cheap and sleazy bar in the county, both as a member of the band or as a patron.

"Those are the kind of places we hung out, so that's where our band played. When we first started the band, we had high hopes of being rich and famous, but it didn't happen. The party atmosphere quickly took over, and we slid right into it. The drinking. And yes, the drugs, too. With all that, Zac sank lower and lower, until I didn't know him anymore." Looking back, she wondered how well she knew herself at that time in her life.

Adrian flinched, but otherwise didn't move. "I don't know if this is a stupid question, knowing you ran away, but do you still love him?"

Celeste shook her head. "No. Not at all. I know I'm not supposed to hate anyone, but when I tried to talk to him about some of the changes that were going on in my life, he said some really horrible and nasty things. I quit drinking and everything else, and then he started getting rough. I guess he saw that I was starting to pull away. I don't know how he thought that being that way would make me change my mind, but he's so far gone I don't know what he thinks anymore. I was scared, so I started looking for a job when he didn't know what I was doing. As soon as I found something, a friend of my mother's helped me find a place to live, and I left. But now Zac's found me, and he's really mad and that's why I'm here. I guess that's my life in a nutshell."

Adrian uncrossed his arms and walked the few steps between them. He was close enough to reach out and touch her, if he wanted to, but his hands remained at his sides. "He started getting rough? Did he hurt you?"

Celeste shook her head. "He didn't leave bruises, and it only happened once. But I knew that once it started, it probably wouldn't stop, not with the way he always let his temper get out of control. If I had stuck around, it would only have gotten worse. So I didn't stick around. It's not like we were married. He never even bought me a ring."

Adrian glanced over her shoulder toward the living room window. "If he's dangerous and there's a chance he's still out there, I think we should call the police."

Celeste felt herself relax just a little. She hadn't given Adrian all the details she had given Pastor Ron, but she'd told him enough to let him know the type of person she'd been before they met. After the excitement was over and she was sure Zac was gone, Adrian would have time to think about what she told him.

Now, all Celeste could do was pray.

Unable to look at Adrian, she turned to face the window. "That's probably a good idea. I was starting to call the police, but when Zac broke the glass…" She turned back, because even though fear sat like a rock in her stomach, she had to see Adrian's reaction. "…that's when I ran."

Adrian stiffened. "What do you mean, 'starting' to call?"

"I dialed, but I didn't actually speak to anyone. When I heard the glass shatter, I dropped the phone and jumped out the bedroom window. I don't think I broke the phone, but even if I did, I don't care. I can buy a new one."

Adrian's eyes widened. "You jumped out the window?"

Celeste nodded, then shook her head. "Sort of. I didn't go far. I only jumped as far as the apple tree. I had to climb down really fast. I've never climbed a tree before, but I don't know if it's still called climbing when the only direction you're going is down."

Adrian leaned closer. Very slowly, he touched her cheek, which stung at the contact. She flinched, but otherwise didn't move.

"Except for a few scratches, you don't seem to be hurt, although I don't know why not. We have to get back to your place right away. They record everything when you call 911. If they heard trouble over the phone, they would have dispatched someone, and they're probably out there searching your house right now and wondering where you are."

Celeste froze. "I heard Zac yelling and swearing and banging things when he was looking for me, before I got to the ground. If the police are there, they might think they're looking for a dead body. Zac was very, very angry. When he went into the bedroom, he at least knocked my lamp off the end table."

She shuddered inwardly. Zac truly had made a lot of noise, which must mean that he knew no one was home on the other side of the duplex. İt scared her to think that he knew. Yet, the alternative was even more frightening. If he didn't know there was no one home next door, that meant he didn't care if anyone was listening to his tirade.

Her stomach rolled, and she wondered if she might throw up.

Adrian looked down at his bare feet. "I'll be right back," he mumbled, and left her waiting in the kitchen. When he returned he was wearing socks.

He handed her a pair of balled-up socks. "Your feet must be cold. I'm sorry I didn't think of that sooner. I don't have any shoes that would even come close to fitting you, but the socks will at least keep your feet warm.

Celeste felt her cheeks heat up as she sat in one of the kitchen chairs and tugged the socks onto her cold feet while Adrian put his shoes on. She didn't know why such a thing would have been embarrassing after what she'd just told him, especially when she was wearing his bathrobe, but she felt awkward.

He didn't say a word during the drive to her house.

Just as Adrian had predicted, a police car with lights flashing was parked in front of it.

Adrian turned off the motor, then escorted her into the house. Once she identified herself as the absent occupant, the attending officer introduced himself as Officer Jacobs. After she explained briefly that it was her ex-boyfriend who had broken in and that she was safe and unharmed, they all walked through the house together.

The damage she had feared was indeed a reality. Furniture and shelves were knocked over, and many items were broken. Strangely, the only thing that seemed to be untouched was her purse, which didn't really matter. Except for holding her ID, she had no money in it.

Officer Jacobs took notes and a few photos as they investigated all the rooms. "Because you know who did this and you have a past relationship you can lay charges of willful damage. If you dialed 911 they taped everything that happened until he smashed the phone, whether you were on the line or not. If he was yelling out threats and you can identify the voice on the tape, I recommend that you get a restraining order. But I'd like to give you another suggestion."

Because Celeste had seen Zac lose his temper before, she could picture him on his path of destruction, breaking her things that now lay shattered on the ground. Between her fear of Zac's retribution, and the fact that his actions had forced her to reveal what she hadn't wanted Adrian to know, Celeste couldn't speak to respond. If she did, she knew she would start to cry.

When she was silent too long, Adrian replied for her. "As long as it will keep her safe."

Officer Jacobs stopped. He tapped his pen to his lower lip as he spoke. "There are never any guarantees with a restraining order, but if you file charges the court can make it a condition of his release that he stay away from the residence, stipulate a distance like, say, one block, and state absolutely no contact. Those types of release orders make it easier to re-arrest stalkers and creeps who can't seem to stay away. Many ex-boyfriends and ex-husbands will breach a release within twenty-four to forty-eight hours.

If this Zac does, we can immediately arrest him, and make it stick as a breach of the conditions set forth."

Adrian stayed silent for a couple of minutes. "I think that's a good idea, if you say that's what works best. But I still think it would be a good idea for her not to be out alone, especially at night, just in case, right?"

"Yes, though at least tonight we don't expect him to come back. Generally with these kinds of things the perpetrator doesn't return immediately after. You don't have to make a decision immediately, but you should within twenty-four hours." He reached into his pocket for a card. "Call me as soon as you decide, and we'll set up a meeting where you can sign all the documents. In the meantime, I'll contact 911 and advise that the tape will be required for evidence. That way they'll make a copy as an exhibit for court and it won't be destroyed."

Celeste nodded as she accepted the card. She didn't want to have to air her dirty laundry in court, but if that was what it would take to keep Zac away, then she didn't have a choice. "Thank you. I'll let you know."

Adrian looked around the living room, surveying the knocked-over lamp and broken CDs. "What about the mess?"

Officer Jacobs tucked his notebook and camera into his pocket. "I've got all the department will need. You'll have to call your insurance broker. They usually won't send anyone to fill out a report if the police have already been to the scene, so they'll just tell you to clean it up and itemize what has to be fixed, and what needs to be replaced."

Celeste stared blankly at the mess. The rush of adrenaline that had kept her going disengaged, leaving her feeling like a soggy dishrag, standing amongst the ruins of her

living room, wearing only her pajamas, Adrian's bathrobe
and socks.

A little voice echoed inside her head.

I can do all things through Him who strengthens me.

All she needed was enough strength to make it twenty
more minutes. Then, when she was alone again, she could
break down and no one would know except herself and
God. "Thank you, officer. I'll think about what you said."

Officer Jacobs turned to leave. "You'll want to cover that
broken window with some plywood or something before
you go to bed. Goodnight. And good luck."

Together, Adrian and Celeste watched Officer Jacobs return to the car. He turned off the flashing lights, said something on the radio, then drove away.

Everything was over. She was safe, but it was time to
get on with her life.

Celeste turned to the gaping hole and the broken glass.
The front area of the house had cooled considerably, and
colder air continued to drift in through the opening. She
felt the chill, both inside and out.

"I don't know what to do. I don't have plywood or anything, and Hank isn't home."

Adrian stepped forward and ran his finger along the
window frame. "I have some in the garage at home. I can
put in something that can make do until Hank can replace
the window. This is supposed to be a special glass that's
hard to break."

"I'm guessing he came prepared."

"What kind of man is this? He obviously had this
planned. You say he times his break-ins to three minutes.
Is he a professional thief?"

"He doesn't think it's stealing when he breaks in to places and takes what he says people owe him. He takes payment in goods, rather than money, if that's what people have. You'd be shocked to know what people will sell when they want their drugs badly enough."

Adrian's finger stopped moving. "Drugs? Your ex-boyfriend sells drugs?"

The room suddenly became colder. "Even before I became a Christian, I told him not to deal. I told him the band earned us enough income, but Zac always wanted more."

"Did he still time his break-ins to three minutes when he was stealing already-stolen goods from other thieves for drug debts?" The sarcasm in Adrian's words was so thick it nearly dripped.

The inner cold degraded to a stark numbness. She hadn't thought things could get any worse, but they were spiraling out of control exponentially. Being with Zac and knowing where the money came from made her equally as guilty as Zac.

"Believe it or not, people who have stolen property that they're using will still call the police when they figure someone is trying to steal from them. I know it's wrong, but if it's not sitting somewhere obviously waiting to be sold, they figure it's theirs and they will protect it. As long as there aren't any drugs currently on the premises, they'll call the police. So yes, he times it."

She turned to Adrian.

"All that is behind me. I tried to convince Zac what he was doing was wrong, but he wouldn't listen. I didn't want to live with him anymore. I quit drinking, I quit taking drugs. I even quit performing, because standing up there half naked and singing those garbage songs wasn't pleasing to God. As soon as I found a job and a place to live I got out of there, and I haven't looked back. Isn't that enough?"

"I didn't say anything. It's not up to me to sit in judgment."

It wasn't, but there was no doubt about it; the life she had led up until a very short while ago was very, very wrong. Even for an unbeliever, it was wrong.

Adrian stepped back. "I'll go get some wood and something to put it up with. You'll be safe. There are people still outside, standing around watching. I'll be right back."

Suddenly, with Adrian gone, she felt more alone than she ever had in her life, even more alone than on the days after she first ran away from Zac and all that went with him.

Celeste probably should have run upstairs to change, but she couldn't move. Instead, she shut her eyes and prayed for forgiveness as she'd never prayed before. She knew God had forgiven her for all she'd done, at least in theory. She knew that as a Christian, Adrian was supposed to be forgiving, even if what she'd done wasn't against him personally. Instead of feeling released, the weight of every sin and every rotten thing she'd ever done sat heavily on her shoulders, threatening to crush her or drown her, she didn't know which.

Adrian returned and worked in silence. Within minutes an ugly but functional piece of plywood covered the gaping hole in the broken window.

"That should do until Hank can replace it properly."

"Thanks, Adrian. For everything. I don't know what I would have done tonight without you."

It was true. There had been no question in her mind

about where to go and who to seek out. She needed Adrian to be her sturdy pillar of strength. Just as she knew he would, Adrian supported her when she was weak, and stayed with her until she got her bearings back.

Celeste turned to the night sky. In a few hours it would be daylight, and both of them needed some sleep in order to face the day.

The wake of Zac's reappearance had to be dealt with. Their plans to go to the library had to be discarded. The considerable mess would take an entire day, if not more, to clean up. Officer Jacobs had told her to take notes of everything that was broken, in case there was something they hadn't noticed or recorded on their initial check, and that would slow the process even more.

She didn't want to ask Adrian to help clean up Zac's mess, but she couldn't right all the furniture herself. More than needing Adrian's physical strength, she needed him.

So far, he'd stayed at her side. He'd been the strong one, but right now, at this moment, she needed to hear him say that nothing had changed from earlier in the day.

Celeste held her breath while she recalled how sweet he'd been in the restaurant parking lot. The romantic turn to whatever was happening between them had felt wonderful and had scared her to death at the same time. However, instead of encouraging him or even being receptive, she'd all but shut him out. Still, she knew what he had wanted to say—that he cared for her, maybe even loved her.

Now, she wanted to hear those words more than anything in the world, but she knew she wasn't going to hear them. Despite his earlier near-declaration, right now she wasn't sure if he still wanted to be friends, much less more.

If she could turn the clock back, she would run into his arms, hold him, sink herself into his warmth, and never let him go.

Despite the time and her exhaustion, Celeste wanted to ask him to stay a little longer to keep her company. However, once she opened her mouth, she knew that if he showed any hesitation, she would quickly deteriorate from asking into begging. But begging wasn't necessarily a bad thing.

Beside her, Adrian didn't move except to turn his head to stare at the devastation of her living room. His voice came out in a flat monotone. "Do you have any insurance?"

His voice sent a cold chill down her. Celeste clutched Adrian's bathrobe tightly around herself and tried not to look at the mess, or the plywood-covered window. She forced herself to speak, but her voice came out barely a whisper. "No."

Adrian spun around so his back was toward the downed shelving unit. "I'll call the guys when daylight comes and see if they can help."

Before she could say anything else, he was gone.

He didn't say goodbye.

She didn't know if he was coming back with the other guys.

She knew she wasn't being fair, but she couldn't help it. She wanted him, but she couldn't have him. He deserved someone better than her, but she didn't want to let him go.

Unless he left, all by himself.

Chapter Thirteen

"On three. One, two, three…"

With Bob on the other side, Adrian pushed the bookshelf upright, then back into place against the wall.

Adrian wiped his hands on his jeans. "That thing is heavier than it looked. I wonder how she got it there in the first place."

Bob swiped one hand through his hair. "It comes in pieces, and you add one section at a time. None of the parts are heavy by themselves, but when you put it all together, it becomes a nice, solid unit."

"Yeah." Adrian flexed his shoulder. "A *heavy* solid unit."

"I told you before, and you didn't believe me. You're getting flabby with that desk job, my friend."

Adrian grumbled under his breath, knowing Bob really didn't expect a response. Still, it was a sad fact that he was more out of shape than he'd ever been in his life. Ever since he accepted the management position, he'd been more confined to his desk than before, but the desk went with the job.

Until recently, he'd been diligent about walking or jogging once or twice a week, and in the summer time, he rode his bike on the weekends.

This past summer, he could count on one hand the number of times he'd taken his bike out of the garage.

It had started the day he met Celeste.

Adrian stiffened, then glanced around her living room. Her home looked worse in the light of day.

He still found it difficult to believe that one person could wreak such havoc in under five minutes, yet the evidence lay everywhere. Celeste had confirmed that nothing was stolen. Of course, it was quicker to destroy things than to steal them. Also, by acting in this way, her ex-boyfriend had had a more lasting effect than by simply stealing Celeste's belongings. Of greater detriment than having to merely replace missing items, Celeste needed to handle and inspect everything she treasured that was damaged, then discard what could not be repaired. Celeste didn't appear to have any antiques or other pricey treasures, but she did have a number of items of sentimental value.

It would have taken seconds to tip over the bookshelf, but it would take hours, even days, to make it all right, if it could ever be made right. Some things could never be replaced.

Adrian failed to see how someone could do such a thing to another person, especially one they had once loved. Yet, he couldn't deny that it happened. He often saw such things in the newspaper or on television, where a jilted lover resorted to extreme measures for revenge or retaliation.

Adrian's heart skipped a beat.

A jilted lover.

Zac was a jilted lover in every sense of the word. Celeste had admitted that she ran away from a long-term relationship.

Not long ago, Adrian had bluntly told her that he was seeking a long-term, committed relationship. Now, he didn't know if Celeste's definition was the same as his. When the time came, Adrian intended to seal his commitment of love, honor and faithfulness before God, in marriage, for life.

He had no intention of living with a woman, allowing an easy way for either party to leave if the situation became less than ideal. Adrian was prepared to work at a relationship, with God's help and guidance, to make the union with the woman who would be his wife as perfect as could be. He needed to find someone who felt the same way, shared the same faith—someone who would be true to their vows, devoted to God and to her spouse.

Adrian stared blankly at the devastation at his feet.

He didn't know what kind of man this Zac could be, but Celeste was so frightened of him that she jumped out the window and ran several blocks in her pajamas.

Until yesterday, Adrian had thought they shared the same ideals and similar goals. After experiencing a sample of the type of man Celeste had shared a long-term relationship with, Adrian found it difficult to accept that her standards were so low.

Now, he wondered how well he knew the real Celeste. He'd fallen in love, but had he fallen in love with a mirage?

Adrian turned toward the front door, the entrance area darkened because of the plywood over what was left of the window. He didn't know what kind of force it would take to break through the leaded glass used beside the window, but he thought it would be considerable. If Zac had the strength to break such a window with his bare hands, Adrian didn't want to think of what that kind of force could do to a person. If Celeste was in danger from an abusive relationship with a person like this, then she had every justification to leave Zac, married or not. Indeed, if she'd been living in fear that someone she loved would hurt her, then it was a miracle she trusted men at all, including himself.

In hindsight, he could now make sense of the mixed messages she'd been sending him.

Yet, at the same time, when she'd kissed him, the message there was clear. There had been no hesitation and certainly no fear.

Thinking more of the way she'd kissed him, and the way she'd held him caused his heart to pound and his temperature to rise.

"Adrian? Earth to Adrian. Are you okay?"

Adrian blinked and shook his head. "Sorry, Bob. I was thinking about something else."

Bob looked around at the books, broken CDs, and other items, many of which could be seen also to be broken, now that the bookshelf no longer covered them. "I can only guess. You said her ex did this?"

"Ex-*boyfriend.*"

Bob's eyebrows quirked when Adrian specified what kind of ex he'd been talking about, but Adrian left Bob to figure it out himself. Adrian wasn't up to explaining it.

Suddenly, Adrian felt restless. He didn't want to stand around in the living room doing nothing. He couldn't start cleaning up, because from here, as unpleasant a task as it would be, it would be up to Celeste to sort through her belongings and make her own decisions on what to keep. "I'll go see what Celeste is doing. I think I hear her in the other room with Randy."

On his way to the spare bedroom, he saw Paul in the kitchen, sitting at the table, trying to glue something back together.

He found Randy and Celeste in the spare bedroom. Celeste stood behind Randy as Randy sat on the floor, screwing the computer back together.

"It looks like it's just dented, but we won't know until we turn it on, and we can't do that without a monitor." He looked at the monitor, now sitting upright on the floor, surrounded by the broken glass of the shattered tube. "I think I've got a couple of similar models in the store, but I won't be able to get one to you until Monday night after work. I don't want to wait that long, so if you don't mind, I'd like to take your tower home and test it. If there is something wrong, it might be only connections or small parts that I can do something with, and all my tools are at home."

Celeste's voice trembled as she spoke. "I know you'll be able to fix it. I really appreciate it."

Randy turned his head up and looked at Celeste. "I'm good, but I'm not that good," he said, completely serious. "I hope you've been making adequate backups of all your data."

"Yes. I just hope all my disks are there."

Celeste bent down and picked up a cartoon-character figurine that Adrian had given her, which she'd had sitting on top of the monitor—when the monitor was on the desk instead of in pieces on the floor. "I'm glad I didn't tell him I was going to night school. If Zac knew I was trying to improve my life, he would have completely destroyed the computer rather than just kicking it and knocking the monitor off the desk." With a start, Celeste turned around. "Adrian. I didn't see you come in."

Adrian cleared his throat. "You can't tell if it's going to work?"

Randy shook his head. "Nope." He stood. "If you'll excuse me, I think I need some coffee. I guess you don't have any donuts hanging around?"

Celeste smiled weakly, for the first time that day Adrian suspected. "No, no donuts, Randy."

Randy shrugged his shoulders and left without further comment.

After Randy was gone, Celeste turned to Adrian. "Thanks for getting everybody together. I don't know what I would have done without everyone here."

Adrian rammed his hands into his pockets. "Yeah, well, that's what friends are for. I heard you telling Randy that you didn't tell Zac you were going to night school. You've obviously been talking to him recently. I thought you told me you ran away from him."

She looked up at him, her eyes big and wide and very sad. "He saw me at the bank last week at lunch time. He wanted to talk, so I met him for lunch at the taco stand twice. I was very careful not to tell him anything about what I've been doing or where I lived. That's the reason I left my mom's car at work and found alternative transportation. I guess I didn't do as good a job as I thought. On Friday I told him I was happy and I didn't ever want to see him again. I think this is his way of getting back at me. Now he's got his revenge."

"You should go to the police station and do what that police officer said."

"I don't know. This is pretty final."

"I wouldn't be too sure of that. If this is the kind of thing he does, that means he's unpredictable, and that makes him even more dangerous."

"I should have seen this coming, but you're probably right. I guess I should lay charges, as the police officer said."

"Then let's go now, while everything is still fresh in your mind. I'm sure that someone else can do the paperwork for you if Officer Jacobs isn't there."

She glanced to the doorway. "But what about the guys?"

"I think everything is pretty much done except for the things you have to go through on your own. They can leave now. They'll understand. In fact, I'm positive they will all want you to have the restraining order, too."

"Okay. I have to change, though."

"That's fine. I'll go tell them what we're going to do."

He left before Celeste had a chance to question him about the *we*. She could have gone alone, but he wanted to hear more, to fill in what she'd left out when explaining everything to him, because there were a lot of blanks. His stomach churned at the pictures that were shaping up in his mind. Of all his preconceived notions, he didn't want her really to be that bad.

He sat at the table as Paul tightened the lid on the glue.

"Where's Randy and Bob?"

"They left. What's up?"

"I'm going to take Celeste down to the police station right now. Thanks for coming over on such short notice to help."

Paul shrugged his shoulders. "Not a problem. What are you doing tonight? Do you want us to come back?"

"No, Celeste has to decide what she's going to keep, and what needs replacing by herself. I think I'm going to make a little trip to the wild side tonight."

"Come again?"

"I want to see what this Zac looks like. She told me Zac has moved since she left him, so she doesn't know his current address. The only real job he has is playing in bar bands, so he doesn't exactly have a work address, either. But he did tell her where he's going to be playing for the next month, so she has an address for the police when they present him with the restraining order. I'm going to check it out."

Paul's eyes widened. "Bar bands? You're going bar hopping?"

"Not hopping. Just to one bar, for one night."

"I hope you're not thinking of confronting this guy. After seeing what he did here in just a few minutes, I don't think you're any match for him. He threatened her, too, so he's obviously the type that resorts to violence quickly."

Adrian rested his hands on his stomach, remembering Bob's comments about how out of shape he'd become, and how Celeste had told him that she'd had to pay Zac's bail when he was arrested for fighting. In order for the police to have been called, it had to have been a serious fight. Zac must have been victorious if he'd only been taken to the lockup rather than the hospital, where his opponents were sent.

But Adrian had to see the type of life Celeste had led before they met. He wanted to know the real Celeste. There was only one way to learn, and that was to go.

"I have no illusions of superhuman strength or a sudden knowledge of martial arts. I know when I'm out of my league. I'll have a quick look and then leave."

Paul turned his head and scanned the mess that still remained in the room. "I don't know if that's such a smart idea. I'm going with you."

Adrian opened his mouth to protest, but then snapped it shut. He didn't really want to drag his friend into such an environment, but he also didn't look forward to going alone into the unknown. "I appreciate it. I'll pick you up at six."

"Amen!" Pastor Ron called out to the congregation.

"Amen!" the congregation replied.

Adrian watched for Paul's signal, and they all started playing the closing hymn, ending another Sunday service.

He was glad it was finally over. All through the service he'd been more distracted than he'd ever been before.

He'd spent most of the worship time watching Celeste. Studying her. Analyzing what should have been a private time for her, even though they were on the stage for the entire congregation to watch.

Guilt poked at him, but he couldn't stop.

Just like the worship team, Zac's band had consisted of four people, a man each on guitar, bass guitar and drums, and a woman on the keyboard.

The woman playing the keyboard looked nothing like Celeste, or at least like the Celeste he knew. He'd seen more fabric covering women in the underwear section of catalogues than was covering the body of the woman on stage.

Celeste's words echoed in his head.

"...standing up there half-naked..."

At the time, he'd thought Celeste had been exaggerating, but to say the woman who had been her replacement was only *half*-naked was being generous. He suspected Celeste had dressed in a comparable manner. The lyrics of the songs he'd heard had been filled with more coarse language and suggestive phrases than anything he'd ever heard on the radio.

And then there was Zac. After listening to Celeste describe Zac when she filled out the police report, he had no trouble determining which of the three men was Zac.

If he had had any doubt, when Zac stepped up to the microphone to introduce himself and the band, Adrian heard the same voice as he'd heard in the obscene phone call made to Celeste's house.

Adrian closed his eyes and shuddered. Even without hearing Zac, or listening to Celeste's description, Adrian would have recognized Zac immediately. He'd already seen him once before.

One recent evening, when Adrian had walked to Celeste's house instead of driving, he'd seen a man walking slowly in front of Celeste's house. The man hadn't done anything to indicate that he'd been particularly interested in Celeste's house, but his appearance had nearly stopped Adrian in his tracks. The man wore jeans so tight Adrian didn't know how he could walk comfortably. His starkly dyed white-blond hair contrasted vividly with his completely black clothing. Multiple piercings, many of which looked painful, had also caught Adrian's attention.

From the stage, those things made Zac exude a 'bad-boy' attitude and arrogance, which some women probably found enticing. But on the typical residential street in their quiet suburban neighborhood, Zac had appeared tough and downright creepy.

In hindsight, Adrian kicked himself for not telling Celeste, but he truthfully hadn't connected the man whom he now knew as Zac with the phone call or with the man he'd seen on the street. Perhaps it wouldn't have made any difference anyway. After that day, it had seemed likely that Zac had done his surveillance more unobtrusively; Adrian hadn't seen him since. It had been easy to forget.

It had sat like a lump of coal in Adrian's stomach to see Zac play guitar, so similar to his own playing, yet in such a radically different setting.

He hoped and prayed he had nothing else in common with Zac, who had been the first man in Celeste's life.

The band had been very together when they performed, but when the music ended, not one of them could walk in a straight line. Every member of the band was obviously under the influence of something probably illegal, but no one present cared. In fact, many of the other people in the bar, both on and off stage, also appeared to be affected by something. Adrian had never felt so uncomfortable in his life. Paul had commented that he hoped none of the children he'd taught in school over the years turned into anything like what they'd seen.

Adrian knew he shouldn't judge people by the company they kept, but after watching Zac and the goings-on at the bar, it was difficult to keep an open mind. For many years, by her own admission, Celeste had been a willing and active participant in everything he'd witnessed. But by condemning Celeste, he was going against what God commanded. Yes, people were to be held accountable for their sins, but God was the only one who could judge. Adrian led a good life, but he was by no means sinless. He had no right to judge Celeste, regardless of what she had done, or his interpretation of it. Yet he didn't know what to make of all of it.

Once again, he tried to push the thoughts out of his mind, knowing they would haunt him again and again. He turned his concentration onto what he should have been doing in the first place, which was tidying up the stage so the ladies' group could use it for an afternoon meeting.

When Adrian joined everyone for lunch after the service, he didn't say much. Instead, he sat back, watched and mostly listened. He noticed that Celeste wasn't doing much talking, either. Instead, Randy more than filled in the gaps, entertaining them all with tall tales and obvious exaggerations of his life in the past week.

This time, Adrian didn't invite Celeste to spend the day with him, nor did she ask him.

After the evening service, he dropped the electric piano off at her house, just as usual, but he didn't stay. He went home. When he couldn't concentrate on the book he was reading, Adrian watched a few reruns on television, then went to bed.

He didn't know the woman he'd fallen in love with.

For the first time in his life, even though he'd lived alone for years, he felt truly lonely.

Chapter Fourteen

Celeste inhaled deeply, and knocked on Adrian's door. It was Wednesday night, their scheduled practice. She didn't want to be there, but she couldn't not go. Adrian was the one good, constant thing left in her life, and she felt him slipping away.

She didn't want that to happen, but she didn't know what she could do to prevent it.

The door opened. Adrian smiled hesitantly, looked over her shoulder to confirm that she was alone, then stepped aside. "You're early."

"I know. I thought we should talk."

Adrian checked his wristwatch. "Sure. Would you like some coffee?"

"No, the rest of the guys are going to be here soon."

She followed him into the living room. Instead of sitting on one end of the couch as he usually did, Adrian sat in the recliner. Sitting alone on the large couch made Celeste feel even more set apart.

Celeste cleared her throat, and tried to sound casual. "You missed Bible study on Monday. Were you sick?"

He shrugged his shoulders. "Not really. I was just too tired."

Celeste cringed. He hadn't missed a Monday-night meeting since she'd known him. If he didn't go because he knew she was there, then that was her fault for not giving him the space he needed. If he didn't go because he really was too tired, it was because he hadn't slept well on Sunday night. That was her fault, too. After everything that happened on the weekend, she hadn't slept well, either.

"I missed you after night school yesterday." It had felt odd to come home after classes and not see Adrian there. She'd given him a key, and most Tuesdays and Thursdays, when he hadn't insisted on driving her to school and then picking her up, he was at her home with a nice pot of tea ready and waiting. Just in case she needed help, he claimed, even though she seldom did, and they both knew it. What usually happened was that Adrian simply sat in the living room with a book while she went through her notes. It just felt good for him to be there, and she liked to think he felt the same way.

"I thought if you had a problem, you'd phone."

She waited for him to continue, hoping he would say that she should have called. Silence hung between them like a timeless void.

She couldn't stand it. "Randy managed to fix my computer. He also found a new monitor for me. It's not as good as the other one, but it works, and it's good enough for my needs."

"That's good."

Again, she waited, but he didn't say anything more.

The back of her eyes burned, and her throat became so tight she didn't know if she could speak, even if he suddenly did say something that needed a response.

Her worst fear had come true. The connection they shared was gone. She had dreaded the day he would know everything, but now that it had happened, reality was far worse than her fears. She'd always known she wasn't good enough for him, but she'd been like a hungry little bird, following behind Adrian, scooping up any crumbs of friendship he offered. Now that he knew everything, there were no more crumbs. Adrian, being the way he was, would always be nice to her, but the bond was broken.

Now that Adrian knew, it didn't matter who found out. Yet, the first people to know should be her friends. The only other friends she had. If they still wanted to be her friends.

"I guess I should talk to the guys."

"That's probably a good idea."

She lowered her voice, forcing the words out. "I don't know what you've told them so far."

"I told them that Zac is your ex-boyfriend, and that's all. It's not my place to say anything. It's up to you. Although, Paul knows I went with you to get started on the restraining order."

She gulped, then continued. "I'd really like to remain on the worship team. I know I don't deserve to be up at the front, because I'm not a very good example for everyone, but it's something I really like to do. God saved me in so many ways, and being on the worship team is a small way that I can do something for Him. I want to help everyone worship God better. But I don't deserve to be up there."

"All have sinned and fall short of the glory of God, Celeste."

"That's true, but now you know that I fall a lot shorter that everyone else."

His lack of a reply confirmed what she already knew. She fell short, not only in God's eyes, but also in Adrian's.

"I'm pretty sure that everyone will say you still belong on the worship team. Unless you haven't been faithful to God."

"You know me better than that."

He sighed. "I thought I did know you, but if we're going to be honest with each other, I'm not so sure any more. To find out where you've been and some of the things you've done has really come as a shock to me, especially when I had to fill in a lot of the blanks at the police station. I'm not sure I know the real Celeste. Don't you think you should have told me before I had to find out the hard way?"

Celeste froze. If the situation were reversed, she would have felt the same way. She hadn't lied to him, but she certainly hadn't told him the truth. She'd deceived him by letting him think things she knew weren't true, only because she was afraid. In the end, because she'd waited and buried her head in the sand, the situation snowballed. The way he'd learned was worse than if she had actually told him. She couldn't blame anyone else for how Adrian felt, not even Zac.

Her voice lowered to barely above a whisper. "I've asked myself that a thousand times since we met. There never seemed to be a good time to tell you."

"Look, Celeste, I want to be completely honest with you. Paul actually knows more than just the restraining order. We've seen Zac."

Celeste's stomach did a nosedive into her shoes. "When did you talk to him? What did he say? Did you talk about me?"

Adrian held his palms up toward her. "Not so fast. I didn't say I talked to him. I only watched him. From a distance. I took Paul to where you said Zac was playing on Saturday night. I had to see him."

Celeste didn't know whether to laugh or cry. Either way, she felt as though she was going to throw up. "Why?"

Adrian sighed, folded his hands together in his lap, and stared down at them, not looking up at her as she spoke. "I don't know, exactly. Of course I wanted to see the kind of man who would do such a thing, but there's more to it that I can't explain. I don't even fully understand myself. I only know that I was driven to see him, to know what he was like, because seeing him would give me more of an insight on you."

Celeste felt as if she'd been tried and convicted without a jury. If Adrian had seen Zac and the band, then Adrian had seen exactly how bad she had been. Her replacement would have been wearing clothes she had once worn and following Zac's instruction on how to behave, exactly as Celeste had done before her. The drugs and booze freely floating around the bar also spoke loud and clear.

It was a world where the more depraved a person became, the more they were used as an example of what to become. Everything there was the exact opposite of everything Adrian lived for.

Celeste rose and forced her next words out, even though it felt as if she were sounding her own death knell. "Then I understand if you don't want to…" she gulped, searching for the right words, which didn't come. "...be friends anymore." She turned toward the door, but Adrian sprang out of his chair and blocked her path.

"No, Celeste, don't go. I want to be fair, but this has all been a lot for me to digest. I need more time to let everything sink in. I have to work it out."

Before she could ask him how long he needed, the doorbell rang. Adrian hadn't taken more than three steps when the door opened and Randy entered without waiting to be let in. "Hey, Celeste. Did you get everything straightened around?"

"I suppose."

The door hadn't closed, and Paul and Bob walked in, making Celeste suspect that the three of them had met for dinner before the practice. She also suspected that she'd been the main topic of conversation.

That meant there was no time like the present.

"Before we start, I thought I should tell you guys why my ex-boyfriend trashed my place." She closed her eyes, picturing the destruction, which was even worse in the daylight. "It's because I left him and the lifestyle that went with him. I told you when we first met that I hadn't been a Christian long, but what I didn't tell you was that before I became a Christian, I spent most of my time in the bars. My job was as the keyboardist for a bar band, and it also was my social life. With that went everything else. I'm sorry I didn't tell you sooner. I didn't mean to deceive you, but I was too afraid to tell you."

A silence hung in the air before Paul finally spoke.

"After Saturday night, when I went to the bar with Adrian, I assumed most of that. We've already talked about it before we got here." He turned to Adrian. "Except we haven't talked to Adrian. I hope you don't mind."

Adrian shrugged his shoulders and remained silent. She could only imagine what he was thinking.

"All that matters is what you believe now, and how you've been leading your life since you made your decision to follow Jesus. If what you've done and how you've acted since then has been okay with God, then it's certainly okay with us. We're not going to kick you off the worship team or anything like that. All have sinned. All of us. That includes me, Bob, Randy and Adrian, too. But we're forgiven when our hearts are in the right place when we ask." He turned once more to Adrian. "Right?"

Adrian had said the same thing to her only minutes ago, but the words didn't mean the same thing when directed at Adrian. Celeste doubted Adrian had done anything bad in his life, certainly nothing illegal or self-destructive.

Celeste felt lower than an earthworm. Even the earthworms lived a better existence than she had. They were at least true to the way God made them.

Bob and Randy both nodded. Adrian remained still. After a few seconds, all he said was, "Of course."

Paul smiled and held out his hands. Celeste reached forward and their hands joined. Paul's touch was the most comforting thing anyone had done since her life had imploded. The backs of her eyes burned, but she blinked quickly so she wouldn't embarrass herself any worse.

Paul gave her hands a gentle squeeze. "Great. Then let's get started. I've picked a new song, so we've got a lot to do in a short amount of time."

The practice progressed well, just like any other practice, for which Celeste was infinitely grateful.

When Randy, Bob and Paul left for the kitchen to get their donuts, Adrian motioned for Celeste to stay in the room.

"You know that word of the break-in is going to get back to the church population. People were standing around wondering what was going on, and word travels fast. I'm sure people are already talking. There will be questions—innocent questions, but there will be questions. I hope you have an answer figured out."

"You mean an answer without going into my sordid history?"

Adrian's lack of a response confirmed that was exactly what he meant.

"It's okay, Adrian. I got myself into this mess, I can get myself out." And if she couldn't get herself out, then she could always leave. She'd done it before, and it had worked, although leaving the church would break her in two.

He nodded. "Good. Now let's go get some donuts while there's still some left."

She shook her head. "If you don't mind, I think I'll pass. I'm really tired." She almost said that she would see him the next day, after classes, but she wasn't sure it was going to happen. Instead, she simply let herself out and went home.

Adrian stood at the window of his office overlooking the expanse of the downtown skyline, and sighed. He wasn't up high enough to see the building where Celeste worked, therefore nothing out the window held his attention.

He returned to his desk and picked up the picture of Celeste from beside the monitor. When he, a single man, first put the picture on his desk, his workmates teased him endlessly, but he brushed them off easily. It was when his office assistant asked him in all honesty about Celeste that he didn't know how to respond. He couldn't even call her his girlfriend, despite the fact that until recently they spent nearly all their time together.

The best he could do was say Celeste was a friend. His secretary must have seen the regret in his admission, because at that point, all teasing stopped.

He stared at Celeste's picture, at her smiling face. It had been taken one day when Bob had dared Celeste to play drums for a song. Randy had taken a picture with his new high-tech digital camera just as Celeste hit the cymbal, then laughed because she hit it too hard. Her hair was a mess from bouncing up and down as she played the drums, and her gorgeous green eyes sparkled with laughter. She looked happy and playful, and incredibly beautiful; he couldn't decide if it was despite her state of disarray, or because of it. The picture was so good Randy had printed it out on photo-quality paper, framed it and given him a copy.

Adrian stared at the picture.

Everything was different now.

Now that he knew the real Celeste.

Or did he?

He squeezed his eyes shut. When he wasn't looking at the photograph, he could only picture Celeste as he had seen the woman in the band, with Zac, at the bar, scantily dressed and belting out lyrics that would make a sailor cringe. Which one was the real Celeste?

"Excuse me, Adrian?"

Adrian opened his eyes to see his office assistant standing in front of the desk. "Sorry, Brittany. Have you got something for me?"

He replaced the picture on the corner of the desk as Brittany handed him a folder. "This needs your signature, and they need the financial statements this afternoon for an emergency stockholders' meeting."

He paged through the file, then applied his signature. "This is all in order. Call the courier and…" his voice trailed off. The address was a block from Celeste's office.

Every new discovery about Celeste had come crashing down on him, in waves. His perception of her had plummeted, based on what he'd seen in the bar, because that's what she said she used to be like.

But was that fair?

No, he told himself. Paul's words echoed through his head. What mattered was how she led her life *now,* not a year ago, not six months ago, not even yesterday.

But he had to know who she was a year ago, in order to understand who she was today.

He had to talk to her, and the best place for that was not at his home, where he had only good memories. Not at her home, which still showed signs of the chaos that had ripped him out of his cozy fantasy. He needed to talk to her on neutral ground.

Adrian stiffened and didn't offer the file back to Brittany. "I have something else in the area to take care of. I'll take it there myself."

"You? But… Okay. I'll call them and let them know."

As soon as Brittany left the room, Adrian opened his e-mail program.

To: Celeste
I think we should talk. I'm going to be in your neighborhood on business later today, and I'd like to take you
out for lunch. My treat.
Adrian

Her reply came in under four minutes.

To: Adrian
As long as it won't interfere with your meeting. I can
meet you at the taco place at 12:05. And I'm paying for
my own.
Celeste

Adrian sighed. He would rather have taken her someplace nicer, but this was neither the time nor medium to
argue with her.

He quickly typed his reply.

To: Celeste
That's fine. See you there.
Adrian

He finished his current file, tidied up his desk, and left
the office, telling Brittany only that he was going to take
some extra time for lunch while he was out.

Traffic was lighter than he expected. Since he had extra
time on his hands, he parked the car at the taco restaurant
and walked to the client's office, then gave the file to the
receptionist quickly, before anyone saw him and wondered

why the Western Regional Manager of their accounting firm hand-delivered an envelope.

Since he was early, Adrian decided to meet Celeste at her office rather than take up a table sitting alone at the taco restaurant.

As he stood waiting for the traffic light, he watched the people around him. Most were obviously people who worked in the area, dressed in casual business attire, but one person across the street stuck out from the crowd.

Black clothes from neck to toe. Shocking white-blond hair. The glitter of too much pierced jewelry.

Adrian's heart nearly stopped.

Zac.

Zac was standing under the awning of the building directly across from Celeste's office, doing nothing else but waiting, and watching.

The light changed. Adrian crossed the intersection, but didn't continue on. He stepped to the side to cross the other way, toward where Zac stood. While waiting for the second light, he alternated between watching Zac and watching the door to Celeste's building.

Unawares, Celeste stepped out of the building. She turned in the direction of the restaurant, and started walking toward where Adrian stood. Adrian quickly turned to see what Zac would do, but Zac was gone. He searched through the crowd of people, watching specifically for the disruption to show that someone was running when everyone else was walking. Everything appeared normal.

Adrian turned and hurried to meet Celeste.

She stopped walking, her eyes widened. "Adrian? What are you doing here?"

"I got finished what I had to do sooner than expected, so I thought I'd meet you at the door instead of sitting alone in the restaurant.

One eyebrow quirked, but she said nothing.

He glanced across the street to the last place he'd seen Zac. It was as if Zac had vanished into thin air, but, of course, Adrian knew that hadn't happened.

He wanted to know where Zac had gone. First of all, he didn't want Zac to watch the two of them together, but more than that, he didn't want Zac lurking, following Celeste. Zac's presence alone was a breach of the restraining order, but Adrian didn't know that saying that he saw Zac for a split second would be enough proof to the police.

He jerked his head in the direction of the restaurant. "Come on, let's get going."

She stepped beside him as they began walking to the restaurant. "Why the hurry? Did you skip breakfast?"

"I never skip breakfast. Breakfast is the most important meal of the day."

"Somehow I knew you were going to say that."

He watched around him as much as he could without Celeste noticing that he was distracted, but Zac was nowhere to be seen.

Once inside the restaurant, they ordered quickly and soon were seated.

"So what brings you down to my end of town?"

"I just had a little business to attend to. So I thought I'd time it in order to have lunch with you."

She didn't respond, but only sat there staring at him, waiting for him to say more.

Finally he couldn't stand it any more. "There is something I have to talk to you about, but it's not the reason I came. Tell me, are you going straight home tonight?"

"I've got school tonight, but after that, of course I'm going straight home. Why?"

"Do you double check the locks on the car doors when you're out? Do you make sure the door is locked when you're driving? Especially at night? I know Bob's done a lot of work on that car, but just in case it stalls, do you have the battery for your cell phone fully charged? Do you have a charger for it in the glove compartment?"

Celeste blinked and started at him. "What's gotten into you? You sound like my mother."

Knowing now what he didn't know then, he wasn't insulted by her accusation. Her mother had to have had some knowledge of Zac and Celeste's situation, and the potential dangers, which had come to pass. Adrian suspected the reason Celeste hadn't stayed at her mother's house initially had been because that would be the first place Zac would look. Also, trading cars had served two purposes—not only did it mean a safe trip for her mother, it also gave Celeste additional anonymity. Except, it hadn't worked. Zac had found her anyway.

"Do you remember when that police officer said that in situations like yours, the offending ex often shows up again, within forty-eight hours? Zac is one of those statistics."

"But he's been warned by the police. In person and in writing."

"He's been here. I saw him just a few minutes ago. Then, the minute you appeared and there was the chance you'd see him, he was gone. I don't know where he went, but I saw him."

"How would you know...oh...I forgot. You've seen him. Are you sure it was him?"

Adrian nodded. "He's pretty unmistakable."

Celeste lowered her half-eaten taco to the wrapper. "I should probably tell the police, but I doubt they'd do anything just because Zac went downtown."

"You're wrong. Zac is supposed to stay two blocks away from you. He knows where you work, so he knows his boundaries. Officer Jacobs said they could arrest him if he breaches the agreement, and he has."

"I think sending the police after him right now would do more harm than good. A fine means nothing to Zac, and they're not going to put him in jail. Officer Jacobs warned me about that. Even if they did, it wouldn't be for long. Then he'd be mad, and you've seen how dangerous and unpredictable Zac can be when he's mad."

Adrian nearly corrected her with the difference between *mad* and *angry,* but stopped himself. In this case, he wondered whether Zac was a combination of both. "Then I should take you to school and pick you up." As soon as the words left his mouth, the overwhelming surge of protectiveness he felt surprised him.

"I don't want Zac to control the way I live my life. I've got to handle this on my own."

"I only want you to be safe."

"I promise you I'll keep the car doors locked, and I'll be sure I don't leave the building alone." Celeste checked her watch. "I have just enough time to get back to work, and my half hour is almost up."

Adrian blinked at her sudden end to the conversation. "Can I walk you back to the door?"

Celeste stood and stiffened from head to toe. She cleared her throat and raised her head high. "You can walk me back to the office, but you can't escort me everywhere I go. I'll manage. I have to."

"Then at least phone me when you get home from school tonight."

"Why? At what point will you decide that something's wrong if I don't phone?"

Adrian gritted his teeth. He was well acquainted with Celeste's defiant attitude, but regardless of her present temperament, she was no match for Zac. He'd seen the results of one of Zac's tirades, and now that he'd actually seen Zac in person, Adrian knew that he wasn't a match for Zac either. The only person he knew who might have the physical strength to handle Zac would be Bob, but Bob didn't know the tricks to successful streetfighting.

"I don't know. I just want to know that you're okay, especially because I know he's out there, watching you."

She shook her head. "I don't think you understand. At some point, you'd draw the line if I haven't called, and then you'd try to find me. But if something was wrong, by then it will be too late, so phoning is pointless. Also, having to phone you to check in all the time makes me just as much your prisoner as Zac's."

Adrian suddenly understood why Celeste doubted the effectiveness of the restraining order, and why she didn't want to anger Zac. Zac acted quickly and secretly. A restraining order gave little protection if all they could do was report Zac as having breached its terms and conditions, especially if Zac confronted Celeste and hurt her.

Adrian's stomach churned. The restraining order would do little good after the fact if Zac raped or killed her.

He didn't know what he could do, but he had no intentions of leaving Celeste open to risk. He wanted to follow her himself, but he knew she would never stand for that. It did make him acknowledge that he wanted to protect her, regardless of anything she'd done in the past.

He stared at Celeste. God promised that He'd forgive anything a person did in the past if they gave their heart and soul to follow Him and do His will.

If God had forgiven her, certainly Adrian could, too. But every time he looked at her, he couldn't let go of what he'd seen in the bar, a mirror of what Celeste once was, including being Zac's partner, for more than just the business of the band.

Still, he couldn't not do anything when she was in danger, whether she wanted his help or not. "I still want you to phone me."

"Fine."

They walked back to her office building in silence. Adrian waited until the glass door closed behind her and she disappeared from his sight inside the building before he began the walk back to the taco restaurant parking lot to retrieve his car, and return to work himself.

The rest of the day passed in a blur. All evening, Adrian paced. He couldn't pray for an answer to how he felt; he could only pray for her safety until she phoned to confirm that she'd arrived at home intact. Until the phone rang, her words echoed through his head. *If something was wrong, by then it will be too late.*

Knowing she was safe allowed him to relax, but when he crawled into bed, he couldn't sleep.

Ever since the day of the break-in, he'd struggled to come to terms with what he'd found out. He didn't know what hurt the most—her background, or the fact that she'd lied to him. Not that she'd really lied, but she certainly hadn't told him the truth.

At the same time he tried to understand why either bothered him so much.

He couldn't help it. He still loved her.

He wanted to put the past behind him, and leave it there, but he couldn't.

Adrian flipped over and did what he should have done days ago. He prayed for an answer.

Chapter Fifteen

"Celeste? There's a man here to see you. He asked if you'd left for lunch yet."

Celeste forced herself to remain calm. She didn't have a job that brought visitors, so therefore the visit was personal. She doubted it was Bob again, because whatever Bob had done to her car, it was running better than it ever had, probably even better than when her father first bought it.

Adrian had been in the area at lunchtime yesterday, so she knew he wouldn't be back two days in a row.

There was only one other person she could think of who might be in the neighborhood.

Zac.

Knowing Adrian had seen Zac watching the door told her that Zac was testing his boundaries. Looking back, despite how careful she thought she'd been to stay inside except for the one day, the only way Zac could have found her in the first place was by watching the exit from the underground parking. Since she was late leaving, the presence of a man asking for her only meant that he knew she was still there.

Celeste cleared her throat. "Is it my mechanic? Can you describe him?"

"He's not the same guy as before, but he's tall, dark and handsome."

Zac was tall. He was handsome, but he wasn't dark, although he had dyed his hair black a few times when the mood struck him. "Anything else?"

"He's wearing a suit to die for underneath a nice overcoat. He's got glasses and beautiful big brown eyes."

Adrian.

Celeste hurried out to meet him. "What are you doing here? This is two days in a row."

He smiled, further accenting those beautiful big brown eyes Sasha had mentioned. Actually, Adrian's eyes were hazel, but for today, *brown* was close enough. "I just happened to be in the neighborhood again, and thought I'd see if you were free for lunch."

"I thought it best for me to stay inside today."

"It's okay. You won't be alone. You'll be safe with me."

She hesitated for just a second. She really did want to go out.

"Okay. Just let me go grab my purse and my jacket."

Celeste headed for the door with more confidence than she'd felt for a long time. For months she'd stayed inside, using the office building like a fortress, to protect her. She'd considered it a haven, but now that she knew Zac had been lingering outside, it felt like a prison.

It wasn't a permanent answer, but for today, being with

Adrian would do. For today, if Zac was out there, he would see that she had at least one big strong friend.

She looked up at him. "Where do you want to go?"

He shrugged his shoulders and held the door open for her. "I thought we could grab a hot dog at the stand and walk around the mall for half an hour where we can get lost in the crowd."

Or where we can be surrounded by hundreds of witnesses, she knew he was thinking, and appreciated the option.

She could feel the stares of her workmates on her back as the door closed behind her. They were going to ask a million questions upon her return, especially since someone was bound to recognize Adrian from the picture she had on her desk.

She remembered vividly the day the picture was taken.

One day at practice, Adrian and Paul had been playing side by side as usual, looking especially spiffy since Paul was left-handed and held his bass guitar the opposite way from Adrian. Dark-haired versus blond, right-handed versus left, Adrian and Paul were picture-perfect together. A few weeks ago Randy had brought his digital camera and caught a perfect photo of Adrian and Paul fooling around. The picture was so good that Randy printed it on photo-quality paper and gave it to her. She couldn't display the picture at home because she didn't want Adrian to see how much she treasured it. Therefore, she took it to work where she could see Adrian's smiling face for eight hours a day, five days a week.

They turned to the left, in the direction of the downtown shopping mall, but they hadn't gone three steps when Celeste's feet skidded to a halt.

She grabbed Adrian's arm, causing him to stop as well. "It's Zac! I see him. There. Across the street!" She pointed, just in case Adrian didn't see him. "And there's some motorcycle thug there with him. What are we going to do?"

Adrian smiled from ear to ear. "We're going to go talk to Zac and the motorcycle thug."

Celeste tugged on his arm, but Adrian began walking anyway. "Don't be stupid. What do you think you're doing?"

"I'm stopping a situation before it gets started. Come on."

Celeste had two choices. She could go with Adrian and confront Zac and his friend, two against two, or she could run back into the office and continue to hide, which so far hadn't done much good.

"God, give me strength," she muttered, not sure if she was praying or begging.

She hurried to catch up to Adrian, praying for courage and the right words as they crossed the intersection together.

As they approached Zac and his friend, Celeste studied the man, whom she didn't recognize from the back. She didn't recognize the motorcycle, either. It was an older model, and it was big. The red paint shone and the chrome glistened. As a whole, the bike was in pristine condition, which was unusual for Zac's friends. As much as the bike was big, it was also noisy, as was any classic bike. The rider revved the motor, then shifted position slightly, almost like a further reminder of his presence.

When they were within three feet, Adrian stopped. Celeste stopped beside Adrian.

Adrian smiled slightly. "Hello, Zac. Bob."

Celeste's heart stopped. Bob?

Bob turned, and smiled at both of them.

It was… Bob. Their friend. On a motorcycle. He'd told her he had alternative transportation when he'd loaned her his car, but he hadn't said what it was.

Adrian turned toward Zac. "Back in the neighborhood again, Zac? Don't think we don't know what you've been doing."

Zac only sneered. "So? The cops will never catch me."

Bob grinned with a lopsided smile. "Probably not, but then the cops won't catch me or my friends either."

Zac's sneer faltered as he looked down at Bob on the motorcycle. Celeste had never seen Bob dressed like this before. He wore tight jeans and a worn T-shirt, accompanied by a well-worn leather jacket that was currently unfastened, despite the chill in the weather. She didn't know how Bob wasn't cold, but she wasn't going to tell him to fasten the jacket in front of Zac. She didn't know where Bob got the jacket, but it had some kind of crest on the back that looked like a gang logo. Yet the jacket fitted Bob to perfection, and he appeared perfectly comfortable in it, as though it was made for him, and as though he wore it often. If she didn't know him, he would have scared her. The whole picture contrasted like day and night with the gentle Bob who was her friend.

Zac turned back to Adrian, and very openly studied him from head to toe.

Adrian stuck one hand in his pants pocket, which reminded her that he didn't have his coat fastened either. His suit would have protected him from the cold autumn day, but Celeste felt cold even with her jacket fastened to her chin. More than the weather, Zac's attitude would have given her chills in the heat of a summer day.

Adrian faced Zac and cleared his throat. "It should be obvious that Celeste isn't interested in you anymore, and she's not interested in your band, either. She's happy where she is, and it's time for you to leave her alone."

Zac turned to Celeste. "You're not really going to give up everything for him, are you?"

Celeste shuffled closer to Adrian until she was pressed up against him. She wrapped her hands around his arm, not caring if she looked clingy. "Yes. I am." She wanted to tell Zac that Adrian was everything he wasn't. Kind. Gentle. Considerate. Adrian also lived his life to please God and help others, while Zac only lived to please himself. The truth was that she would have given up what little she had left for Adrian, if he'd needed it. She loved him that much.

Zac backed up a step. "You haven't seen the last of me," he snapped, then turned and strode off.

Celeste started to shake. She tightened her grip on Adrian's arm, but it didn't help. Her world still swam. After a few large gulps of air, she finally found her voice. "I don't believe this. After all this, all that I've been through, he's gone."

Adrian covered her fingers with his free hand. "For today. I wish I could think of what to do next. I thought confronting him would show him you weren't alone, and that this is a situation he can't win."

Celeste shook her head. "You don't understand. Zac doesn't allow anyone to see weakness in him. If he was going to confront you or strike back, he wouldn't have said anything. He catches his victims unaware, when the mood strikes him. It's a power thing. Everyone is supposed to live in fear of him. It's the only way he gets what he thinks is respect. He said he would be back to make you nervous, so you'll always be watching over your shoulder for him, fearing his return. If he can't get what he wants, in his warped mind, that gives him a partial victory. He sees he's not going to get what he wants, so he made his threat, and left. It's finally over. I'm free."

Adrian released her hand and reached into his pocket. He pulled out a small device not much bigger than a credit card. "I hope you're right. But if you're not, I recorded our conversation on my digital voice recorder, which I'm going to turn over to the police if I ever see him again, for evidence. I think they'd be especially interested in the part about the police never being able to catch him." He turned the unit off, returned it to his pocket, and turned to Bob. "Thanks for holding Zac so I could talk to him—for all the talking I did. I think seeing you is what really got him backtracking."

Celeste also turned to Bob. She swept one arm in the air to encompass the motorcycle and his mode of dress. "What is this? It looks like you're in a motorcycle gang or something. Where did you get all this stuff?"

He smiled and patted the bike between the handlebars. "This is my baby. She used to be my dad's. Isn't she a beauty? I've restored her over the years. I take her out for special occasions, but I also belong to a Christian motorcycle group. We have a retreat once a year, in the summer, where we all camp out in the mountains. And then at Christmas, we have a toy run for underprivileged kids."

Celeste's head swam. "You're kidding…"

His smile widened. "I'm glad I was able to put everything to use to help intimidate Zac. But I've got to get back to work. If I don't see you Saturday, then I'll see you at church Sunday morning." Bob slid his helmet onto his head, fastened the strap, revved the bike, nearly deafening her, and roared off into the traffic.

When he was gone, Celeste sighed. "Don't tell him this, but he didn't have as much effect on Zac as you did."

Adrian's free hand rose up to wiggle the knot in his tie. "I doubt that."

"Seriously. Zac has lots of experience with biker gangs. They don't scare him because he has friends in gangs. He treats gang members with a distant respect, but he doesn't fear them as much as he should. What really intimidates him is someone who can be a success without resorting to threats, violence or intimidation by the number of one's followers. That suit of yours shouts money and success, and your quiet voice shows that you have all the authority you want or need, without having to yell. You say something, you expect people to listen and they do. Zac can compete with bikers and roughnecks, but he's no match for the upper echelons of the corporate universe. Especially since it looks like you've got muscle for backup."

"Really? The guys always tease me about my quiet and uneventful accounting job. I guess I get the last laugh."

She wouldn't have called it a last-laugh situation, and she wouldn't have called Adrian's position as Western Regional Manager merely an accounting job. Also, in Zac's eyes, rather than Bob and Adrian simply being friends, she suspected Zac thought that since they looked so different, with Adrian in his designer suit, and Bob in his gangwear, that Bob and all those that went with him were followers of Adrian. Simple friendship meant nothing to Zac, because his supposed friends would only do something for Zac when there was something in it for them.

But what Zac thought didn't matter. Adrian had come out the winner.

"What was Bob doing here, anyway? And how did he end up talking to Zac?"

"I knew Zac was lurking, so I talked to the guys about it. We all thought it would be a good idea for me to talk to Zac, and then for you to tell him to leave you alone when someone else was with you. Since Paul can't take time off school, and Randy can't take time off from his job at the mall, Bob volunteered to come down to help keep Zac occupied if I caught him lurking again. Since Zac was here yesterday, I suspected he would be back again, today, and he was. But unlike yesterday, today he seemed a little jumpy. I took that as a sign to call Bob and see if he could keep Zac occupied until I could bring you to him and we could tell him together to go away. Bob thought bringing his old Harley would be a nice touch. It apparently worked."

"You left work to come here and watch for Zac, to see if Zac was watching me?"

"Yup."

"What if he had seen you? We were together yesterday, so he would have recognized you."

"So? I wanted to talk to him, anyway."

Celeste stiffened. "Didn't you stop to think of what might have happened if he decided to confront you?"

Adrian shrugged his shoulders. "Then I would have said my prayers and dealt with it. This is the middle of downtown, where a million people would be watching from the high-rise towers."

Celeste stared at Adrian in silence. Adrian wouldn't have known that the only people who could intimidate Zac were corporate-executive types, those whom Zac knew he couldn't bully to get to the top. That was why Zac buried himself so deeply in the dregs, people whose lives centered around drugs and alcohol, thieves and addicts, people who had no other ambition than to survive until the next party on the next weekend. Those were the type of people Zac could control, and he did control them. Those whom he couldn't impress with the scope of his deviousness, he scared into worship by intimidation. Zac had successfully managed to control her until she had learned about the love of Jesus, and that Jesus didn't want her to live that way.

But Adrian wouldn't have known that.

"I can't believe you took that kind of risk." Her voice dropped to a hoarse whisper. "…for me."

"Jesus calls on us to lay down our lives for our friends. Not that I was anywhere close to laying down my life. But I couldn't let this continue to happen, because I was worried that Zac might lose it again, and the next time, what if you didn't get away? I couldn't live with that."

Celeste's heart pounded, waiting for Adrian to expound on his reasoning…that there was no greater love than for someone to lay down his life for his friends, for her…because he loved her.

But he didn't.

It only made sense. The more she came to know Adrian, the more she saw how self-sacrificing he was, and how much he would give of himself for other people. His self-lessness was one of the reasons she loved him so much.

He was such a good, godly person.

And she was…not.

She knew that she wasn't worthy of him, of anything he did for her, especially this latest risk. It was for the best that he didn't love her. It was wrong for someone with a history like hers to fall in love with someone who had probably never done a bad thing in his life.

She shuffled back a step. "You know, I'm not hungry after all. I think I'll go back to the office. I'm kind of behind in my work. I think I'm going to have to stay late and finish up a bunch of things. In fact, I don't think I'll be able to go to the library tonight, even though it's Friday."

"Well…. What about tomorrow? Tomorrow is Saturday."

"I don't know what I'm doing. I guess I'll see you Sunday, then?"

Adrian rammed his hands into his pockets and nodded. "I guess."

Celeste waited for him to say more, but he didn't. In a way, it was a relief.

What he had done only served to widen the gap between them. Now, more than ever, she didn't know what he could possibly see in someone like her, someone who had never done a good thing for anyone in her whole entire life.

If she had any doubts before, she was sure now that the hopes and dreams she had for a future with Adrian were exactly that—dreams. Reality had landed with a harsh thump. She didn't have it in her to be the kind of person Adrian needed to spend the rest of his life with. She was only fooling herself to think it could be any other way.

If Celeste had any doubts before, she was sure now. Adrian's valiant work to rid her of Zac's menace had only proved one thing. They were too different to have any kind of future together. Whatever she hoped to have happen between them, it was over.

Chapter Sixteen

Celeste played an arpeggio, slowing as she reached the high end of the keyboard, then let the resonance of the chord fade away. On cue, all in unison, Adrian strummed one final gentle chord, Paul played one solid but soft low E, and Bob tapped the high-hat cymbal gently, to end the worship time.

They all stepped back from the microphones, but did not leave the stage. Today, Pastor Ron had instructed them to stay at the front. A guest from the ministry board had brought a slide show about overseas missions for the congregation to see. As the presentation ended, he wanted the worship team to play softly while their guest led everyone in prayer, and took up a collection. Then Pastor Ron would continue on with the weekly service.

Randy wasn't able to put the audio clip through the monitors, and they couldn't see the view screen from the stage. However, they had to stay up front because they had to be ready and watch the speaker for the cue to start playing again.

When the lights dimmed, instead of standing center-front on the stage, Celeste tiptoed to the side to wait. Adrian joined her a few seconds later, but Bob and Paul shuffled to the rear, beside the drums, where they leaned against the back wall and started to talk softly.

Not more than a minute passed, and Adrian leaned toward her to whisper in her ear. "You didn't call me yesterday."

Celeste bit her bottom lip. It wasn't that she didn't want to call him. She wanted to be with him more than words could say. After what he did with Zac, she loved him more than ever. However, she could no longer hang on to hopeless possibilities. She'd avoided admitting the inevitable truth for too long, and it was her own fault.

She had no future to share with Adrian. He deserved someone with a background similar to his own, not someone like her. It was because of her that he'd gone to a bar, something he'd never done in his entire life. He'd gone because of her, so it was her fault that Adrian had been tainted once again. He'd only been trying to do a good deed, but because of her, he'd been exposed to something he shouldn't have.

She didn't even want to think of how she'd tempted him physically. She'd done more than simply kiss him, and being selfish, she didn't think of the effect it would have on him until it was too late and she hadn't wanted to stop. Adrian, however, maintained control, and came through victorious, no thanks to her.

"I was busy. I still had a lot of stuff to go through."

"I understand." Adrian looked up at the wall, squinted in the dark, then lifted his wrist and checked his watch. "Pastor Ron said this would take approximately six minutes. That doesn't give me much time, but I want to say this to you now. I have a feeling you're going to run off after the service, and not go out for lunch with the rest of us."

"Well...I..."

"That's what I thought. I wanted to tell you that I sat down with Pastor Ron yesterday and had a good, long talk with him. He helped me sort something out that's been bothering me, and I think you know what it is."

Celeste held her breath. She did know. It was the same thing she'd been fighting herself over. Again, she was a coward. Adrian was going to be the one to say it first. It served her right, but it was better for Adrian this way, that he be the one to tell her it wasn't going to work.

Adrian picked up her hand and gave it a gentle squeeze.

Her eyes began to burn. Even in breaking up with her, he was going to do it gently.

He leaned down, closer, but not close enough to raise anyone's attention if they weren't watching the slide show as closely as they should have been.

"I don't know if I've ever talked to Pastor Ron like that. He actually surprised me. Instead of just listening, he really set me straight. I told him what I was struggling with, and of course he knew who I was talking about. He reminded me that whatever you've done, and no matter how wrong it was, that as long as you've asked God for forgiveness, and you're doing your best to listen to Him and follow His guidance and will for your life now, then you're forgiven. And if God has forgiven you, then I have no right to hold it against you. I'm so sorry, Celeste. I didn't mean to hurt you. I hope you'll let me try to make it up to you."

Celeste had to force herself to breathe. "Wait. *You're* apologizing to *me?*"

Adrian gave a short, very humorless laugh. "Yeah. Pastor Ron told me I was being judgmental, even self-righteous, and it really hit me between the eyes. He was right It's not up to me to judge. That's God's job, not mine. I knew that, of course, but it didn't seem to sink in until Pastor Ron said it. Since you've accepted Christ's sacrifice for your sins, they're gone. God isn't going to judge you. So how can I?"

"But I've done so many bad things."

Adrian gave her hand another gentle squeeze. "All of which have been washed away. It's me that keeps bringing them back, and I have to deal with it. But God forgave you, so, as Pastor Ron so bluntly asked me, who am I to supercede God? I'm so sorry."

"I…"

Paul's whispered voice broke into her thoughts, which were so mixed up she couldn't put two words together anyway.

"Psssttt…. Celeste. Adrian. Come on."

Celeste suddenly realized that Paul and Bob had already taken their places. Celeste and Adrian quickly resumed their positions and watched for the signal to start playing.

The guest speaker's voice droned on while they played in the background, but Celeste couldn't listen to his words. Instead Adrian's apology repeated over and over in her head, to music, while she tried to make sense of it.

She played numbly until it was time to stop, and they all took their seats.

Celeste really tried to pay attention to Pastor Ron's sermon, which according to the notes on the back of the bulletin, was about Moses obeying God, even though Moses didn't think he was the right man for the job.

Moses, who had committed murder, then had run away from all he knew to hide, yet later had become one of the greatest men of God in history.

Celeste's hands began to shake. God had forgiven Moses. Then He had used Moses greatly.

She wasn't Moses. She was a nobody. Less than a nobody.

But she was God's child, just like Moses.

God forgave Moses. And through the blood of Jesus, He forgave her, too.

Just as she had said she would, when the service was over, Celeste went home, but she didn't finish the last of the cleanup.

Instead, she sat in the corner of her living room, and closed her eyes. This time, instead of begging God for guidance, she just sat there and prayed, and listened.

Like the new creation God told her she was.

Celeste pushed the door open and waited for her mother to pass through.

"It's been years since I've been to the library," her mother mumbled. "Why are we coming here, on my first day home?"

"I'm really sorry, I didn't get your e-mail that you were going to be home today. I've had, uh, problems with my computer recently. I have some books that I didn't get returned on the weekend, and now they're overdue. The library closes at six o'clock, so we have to do this before dinner. It won't take long. I hate paying a late fee."

She couldn't believe how much she resented paying the late fee. Not only had Adrian's late-fee obsession rubbed off on her, but he'd also pointed out that when she was late returning a book, that meant that if someone had it reserved after her, they would have to wait even longer to read something she had enjoyed. Since she'd met Adrian, she'd never been late returning a book.

Until now.

Celeste's mother walked past her, through the door and into the lobby. Going to the library with Adrian on Friday night had become a major part of her life. She'd missed two Fridays in a row, and she couldn't believe the void. It wasn't necessarily their long-established routine that she missed. She missed Adrian. Both times, the reason they hadn't gone was because she had been afraid to face him, to hear what she didn't want him to say.

Automatically, she glanced toward the table where they usually sat. Someone else was there, and she almost wanted to ask them to leave, except that it was a public location, open for anyone to use. As well, today was Monday.

The door swooshed closed behind her. The quiet library loomed ahead.

She took care of the fines with the librarian at the desk, then turned around to tell her mother that she was going to take just a minute to pick up something new, but her words caught in her throat.

Instead of seeing her mother browsing at the shelf of new releases, she saw Adrian.

All she could do was stare. Below the hemline of his overcoat she saw tailored slacks that were part of a suit, and leather shoes, meaning that he was on his way home from work.

He reached up to straighten his glasses, then leaned closer to look at something in smaller print on the top shelf.

Even in profile, he looked dashing.

He hadn't called her to ask if she wanted to go to the library with him, but in reality, going to the library wasn't a special event. The only thing that made it special was being together.

After the evening service, she had promised that she would call him when she was ready to talk, and she hadn't.

She continued to watch him. He pulled out a new book he'd been anxious to read. It was a mystery-romance they'd both wanted, and they'd playfully argued about who would get to read it first.

For a few seconds he read the back cover, then opened the book and read the first paragraph. Instead of tucking the book under his arm as he usually did when he picked up something that promised to be a good read, he sighed and in slow motion he pushed it back onto the shelf.

She wanted to talk to him, but she was too afraid. Yesterday, he'd apologized, but he hadn't said anything more. He hadn't said he still wanted her, either in friendship or in any other way. Despite his apology, she knew he was still dealing with how he felt about the way she'd lived before.

As if he felt her eyes on him, he turned his head.

Celeste stiffened.

Their eyes met. Celeste had to force herself to breathe.

"Hi," Celeste mumbled.

"Hi," he muttered, not smiling.

Celeste sucked in a deep breath and stepped closer.

He glanced to the next aisle. "Can we talk?"

No, she thought. She'd spent hours and hours in prayer

since they last talked. After all this time, she'd finally come to terms with the full forgiveness of God. After a tremendous burst of energy, she'd cleaned up every last remnant of Zac's existence in her life, and she was truly ready for a brand-new start. She'd fallen asleep Sunday night in a state of joy and relief such as she'd never known. God had picked her up out of the pit of darkness, and through the sacrifice of Jesus, He'd washed away the blame for everything bad and evil that she'd ever done. She finally could accept that, in every way, fully. She truly was a new creation in God's sight.

But then had come Monday.

She'd had problems at work all day.

When she arrived home, she found her long-overdue car parked in her driveway, and her mother on her doorstep.

When she'd stepped inside her living room, she'd found the note she'd written for herself to return her overdue books.

And now, here was Adrian, at the library. She knew God had truly forgiven her for everything, but as far as Adrian was concerned, she wasn't sure she was quite ready to deal with how he felt. Even though her past was forgiven and she could now put it behind her, it was washed, but not erased. Her past had made her the way she was, and both good and bad, it would still shape her future.

She didn't want to hear that even though he didn't hold it against her, Adrian couldn't live with it, but his past shaped his future, too. He'd only lived a good, Christian life, and she hadn't.

But she needed to put everything of her past behind her. To let it linger would only make it worse. If that meant in-

cluding what she had shared with Adrian, then that was the
way it had to be.

"Yes," she said, "you're right. We should talk. But I
can't be long. My mother's here somewhere, and she's
waiting for me."

He looked up and over her shoulder and scanned the
lobby behind her, but didn't comment.

When his eyes again met hers, Celeste nearly forgot to
breathe.

God had pulled her out of the pit, and when she broke
free to start living the way God wanted her to, the first person He put in her path was Adrian. Adrian had become the
best friend she'd ever had. He picked her up when she was
weak, he made her laugh when she was sad and protected
her when she needed help. She liked to think she did something good for him, even if it was only to shake up his neat
and tidy world and make his life more interesting. They had
their differences, and he wasn't perfect, but he was perfect
for her. She couldn't help but love him.

But could he really love her?

Adrian shuffled his feet, something very unusual for
him. He glanced from side to side, then jerked his head toward the first aisle. "Can we move to someplace a little
more private than this?"

Celeste peeked over her shoulder to confirm that her
mother wasn't behind her somewhere, then followed
Adrian to the first aisle, which was currently free of other
people.

Adrian cleared his throat. "I need to know if you're ready
to stop avoiding me and tell me what's really bothering you."

A million thoughts cascaded through her mind. She

needed to know if he saw her the way she used to be, or the way she was now. She needed to know if it mattered to him what people would think of her, what would happen when she saw people she used to know, or people who had seen her on stage. Did it matter to him that she had nothing—no career, no marketable skills, no nest egg and no friends except her new ones.

Her voice dropped to a ragged whisper.

"Do you remember that night you took me out to dinner? After dinner, we watched the sunset together. It was so romantic that it scared me, and I'm still scared. I need to know if everything you've learned has changed anything from that night. I need to know if you love me…the same way that I love you."

All Adrian's movements stopped. He blinked a few times, then cleared his throat. "I'm not sure." He shuffled a step closer, and picked up her hands, clasping them gently. "I don't know in what way you love me. Are we talking platonic-friendship kind of love, or the other kind?"

She looked up into his beautiful hazel eyes, eyes that were in her dreams and would always be in her dreams.

Her lower lip trembled. "The other kind."

He whispered her name, his hands cupped her cheeks, he lowered his head, closed his eyes and brushed a kiss to her lips.

The awareness of being in the library, surrounded by people, at least on the other side of the shelves of books, faded, as Adrian's arms drifted to her back. He held her tightly and kissed her again, only this time not lightly, and with no hesitation or concern for being in a public place.

Her heart pounded, and she kissed him back with all the

love in her heart. She wanted to keep kissing him, but Adrian being Adrian, he used his usual good judgment and broke the kiss before they were discovered, even though he continued to hold her tightly in his arms. He pressed his lips into her hair, just above her ear, and sighed. It sent warm shivers coursing through her.

"I never want to let you go. I know this really isn't the best time or place to ask, but I have to know. I want to know if you'll marry me. And I'm not talking a long engagement. I'm talking as soon as we can get everything organized."

"M-m-m-marry you?" she stammered. "I never thought that far ahead. Are you sure?"

His arms tightened around her, and his cheek pressed into her temple. "You're everything I've ever hoped and prayed for. My sins are no less short of God's glory. I'm sorry it's taken me so long to see that."

"It's taken me a long time to see that, too."

As if to emphasize that they had both come to the same conclusion at the same time, he gave her a gentle squeeze. She wished she could sink closer into him and never move, but a beep from nearby reminded her that they were in the library, not far from the librarian's desk and checkout counter.

A female voice sounded behind her. "Celeste? There you are, I've been…." The voice trailed off. "What's going on?"

Adrian's right arm fell away, but he held onto her waist with his left, guiding her to his side, and keeping her close.

Celeste felt her cheeks heat up. "Mom…." she stammered, then cleared her throat. "Mom, this is Adrian. Adrian, this is my mom, Kathy."

Adrian held out his free hand. "I've been looking forward to meeting you."

Very slowly, Celeste's mother returned his handshake. "Adrian…. You're one of the men from church Celeste told me about, aren't you?"

Adrian grinned. "I hope so."

The burn in Celeste's cheeks intensified. "Yes. He is."

Celeste gritted her teeth, hoping her mother wouldn't repeat anything else she'd said in her e-mails about Adrian that would embarrass them all. She hadn't told her mother that she had fallen in love, but she'd told her mother much about him, including that he looked great in a pair of shorts.

Her mother scanned him from head to toe, momentarily studied his face, then pointedly stared at his arm, which was still around Celeste's waist.

Celeste cleared her throat. "Mom, we're getting married!"

Her mother's eyebrows rose. "You are?"

Adrian stiffened. "We are?"

Celeste turned her head to look up at Adrian.

His eyes were wide and his eyebrows were raised. In slow motion, as what she'd said sunk in, his mouth turned from being almost being slack-jawed to an adorable, lop-sided smile.

He turned his head and looked down at her, the smile continuing to grow. "Yeah. We are. We're getting married."

Celeste wanted to kiss him again, only not in the middle of the library, and certainly not with her mother watching.

Her mother's eyebrows rose. "I don't know what to say. When did this happen?"

Adrian smiled. "It all started on a hot summer day, when I picked up a stranded motorist on the side of the road."

Celeste tried not to giggle. "Except that's never going to happen again. I've got my car back."

He grinned. "Yeah. And praise God for that." He turned to Celeste's mother. "I think you'll find that car of yours is running much better than the last time you drove it, thanks to Bob." He gave Celeste another gentle squeeze. "The library is about to close. How about if I take both of you out for dinner? We can tell your mother everything, from the beginning."

Celeste smiled. It had been a good beginning. And now, with God's blessings, she was going to have a happily-ever-after ending.

* * * * *

Watch for Bob's story,
HIS UPTOWN GIRL,
book two in the
MEN OF PRAISE *miniseries*
coming in July 2005.

Dear Reader,

Welcome to Faith Community Fellowship! I hope you've enjoyed meeting all the members of the worship team.

I'm a member of the worship team at my church, which is a unique and special place to be. We gather together to praise and worship God, but our practice times are often a special time of prayer, and sharing our special joys or our hurts. Since being on the worship team is special to me, it seemed only natural to tell the story of someone else on the worship team at their church.

Like many church plants, Faith Community Fellowship is small, but growing, partly due to the support and stability of the parent church, where the families of most of the worship team members still attend. These young men have struck out on their own, as we all do when we grow up and make our way in the big world around us.

Like Celeste, sometimes, we make bad decisions. Yet, whatever we've done, God loves us and wants us to come to Him, whether we've known Him and fallen away, or if we are finding Him for the first time. *Hearts in Harmony* is the story of how God met Celeste where she was. He guided her to the people she needed to be guided by, through thick and thin, until she was ready to both be forgiven, and finally, to forgive herself.

When the final pages of Adrian and Celeste's story turned, I found the saga wasn't over. The other members of the team, Adrian's friends, needed their stories to be told. After *Hearts in Harmony*, comes *His Uptown Girl*, where we see loyal and hardworking Bob Delanio taken to where God wants him to be.

I look forward to seeing you again, soon.

Until then, may God bless you in your daily journeys.

gail sattler

Love Inspired

Wedding bells will ring as you enjoy
three brand-new stories in one volume, from
Lyn Cote, Lenora Worth and Penny Richards.
Experience the wonder of falling in love,
along with three women who find happily-
ever-after when they least expect it!

BLESSED BOUQUETS

"WED BY A PRAYER"
BY LYN COTE

"THE DREAM MAN"
BY LENORA WORTH

"SMALL TOWN
WEDDING"
BY PENNY RICHARDS

BLESSED BOUQUETS:
Three touching stories about faith,
friends and the power of love.

Don't miss BLESSED BOUQUETS
On sale June 2005

Available at your favorite retail outlet.

www.SteepleHill.com   LIBB2

LOVING FEELINGS

BY

GAIL GAYMER MARTIN

Calling the police on an eight-year-old wasn't
something Todd Bronski was willing to do…
especially not after he met Jenni Anderson. As
Cory's guardian, she was trying to do the best
for her nephew. Becoming her business partner
meant Todd would spend even more time with the
boy—and his lovely aunt. But Jenni wasn't sure
she was ready to mix business with romance….

Don't miss LOVING FEELINGS
On sale June 2005

Available at your favorite retail outlet.